DONOHUE, David

Alien timebomb

EGMONT PRESS: ETHICAL PUBLISHING

Egmont Press is about turning writers into successful authors and children into passionate readers – producing books that enrich and entertain. As a responsible children's publisher, we go even further, considering the world in which our consumers are growing up.

Safety First
Naturally, all of our books meet legal safety requirements. But we go further than this; every book with play value is tested to the highest standards – if it fails, it's back to the drawing-board.

Made Fairly
We are working to ensure that the workers involved in our supply chain – the people that make our books – are treated with fairness and respect.

Responsible Forestry
We are committed to ensuring all our papers come from environmentally and socially responsible forest sources.

For more information, please visit our website at
www.egmont.co.uk/ethicalpublishing

DAVID DONOHUE

ALIEN TIME BOMB

EGMONT

Also by David Donohue

Walter Speazlebud

Moon Man

David Donohue spent a lot of his childhood
standing in the school corridor for spelling
backwards when he should have been spelling
forwards, and for being a 'cheeky little pup'. As
well as writing for children, David is a songwriter
and a music consultant for film, but he's first
and foremost a backwards speller. And when
he is stopped in the street by people asking
him to spell backwards, he always replies,
'b-a-c-k-w-a-r-d-s', because he's still a
cheeky pup.

For Frank and Eve

EGMONT

We bring stories to life

First published in Great Britain 2007
by Egmont UK Limited
239 Kensington High Street, London W8 6SA

Text copyright © David Donohue 2007
Cover illustration copyright © John Fordham 2007

Photographs copyright © the original photographers

The moral rights of the author and illustrator have been asserted

ISBN 978 1 4052 1999 0

1 3 5 7 9 10 8 6 4 2

A CIP catalogue record for this title is available from the British Library

Typeset by Avon DataSet Ltd, Bidford on Avon, Warwickshire
Printed and bound in Great Britain by the CPI Group

Stnetnoc

Na Noitativni ot Wen Kroy

'This is the news at nine o'clock,' said the voice from the clock-radio, jolting Walter from his dream, the same dream he'd been having for almost a year, ever since his grandad died: he dreamt he was floating helplessly in space while the earth drifted away from him into the blackness. Walter took a deep breath and opened his eyes. The telescope given to him by his granduncle, Bob, sat on a table by the bed and, above his head, Neil Armstrong's lunar boots dangled from a hook. He breathed out – he was not floating in space; he was at home in Nittiburg on the first day of the school holidays.

'Scientists are alarmed by the discovery of a large asteroid on a path towards earth,' said the newsreader. 'If this asteroid, which has been named Hellvega, collides with our planet, humankind as we know it –'

Walter hit the 'off' button with his elbow. He had heard about these so-called 'killer' asteroids before; asteroids on a journey to annihilate the earth . . . but in ten or twenty thousand years! It was all a big yawn. He rubbed his eyes, threw back the duvet, removed the lunar boots from their hook, placed them on the floor and stepped into them. One giant step at a time, he walked towards a small table on which sat a framed photograph of Grandad Speazlebud. How Walter missed him – his crazy humour and his wild, adventurous spirit, his kindness and his big warm heart. And little things too, like how he liked to stick a flower in his lapel when he was going out, preferably a rose he had grown himself.

Beside the photograph lay a small leather-bound book inscribed, Noitanigami by Arnold Speazlebud, and beside that was a small hand-carved wooden box. Walter took the box in his hands and opened it to reveal a gleaming ruby gemstone – the Giftstone, given to Walter by his grandad after he had successfully completed his first journey back in time using the power of **Noitanigami**. He tightened his palm around the box, and with his other hand, opened *The Book of Noitanigami* and read his grandad's introduction:

This gift so rare
Given to you
Can make a million dreams come true
Can stop the arrow-head of time
And send it back, for you and yours
To do the things you might have done
To win the battles you might have won
To right a wrong, or simply be
A witness to Man's history.
When spoken with the power of truth
That nestles in the heart of youth
This gift will cast a blinding light . . .
Then every man will surely see
The power of **Noitanigami**.

Walter felt a gentle heat emanate from the

Giftstone, enter his hands, travel through his entire body and warm his spirit. Just then, as it did most mornings, a Red Admiral butterfly flew in through the open window and fluttered around Walter's head. He fixed his gaze on the butterfly and repeated the word '**Ylfrettub**' three times. The Giftstone glowed as the butterfly instantly reversed its flight path and disappeared out through the window.

'Bye bye, butterfly,' said Walter with a smile.

He enjoyed using his power of **Noitanigami** – sending things backwards by saying their name backwards three times – but he had another power too: the power to travel back in time. Since Grandad had made him Keeper of the Giftstone, Walter could, in theory, time travel on his own, but the mere thought of going back in time without his grandad to guide him had caused him to put time travelling out of his mind.

Walter placed the Giftstone back in its box, returned it and *The Book of Noitanigami* to the table, then clunk-clunked his way across the room to the mirror on the wall. Was he really Walter Speazlebud, the first person on the moon? The answer was yes, of course, but ever since Grandad had gone on his heavenly journey, Walter felt that a part of himself – the adventurous part – had gone for a walk too, and never really come home.

Walter glanced at his 'back-to-front' watch. It said 'm.a. 02.01' (10.20 a.m. to you or me). His kung-fu class started in twenty minutes, and his teacher didn't like it when he was late. He removed Neil Armstrong's boots, hung them back up on the hook above the bed and got dressed.

Downstairs, Walter poured himself a glass of milk and filled a saucer for Maharaja, the green-eyed ginger cat. He remembered the day he had first discovered the power of *Noitanigami*, when he had accidentally said Maharaja's name backwards three times, immediately sending the hapless cat back through the cat flap, across the lawn and up into the apple tree. He smiled, drank his milk in one gulp, grabbed his battered old canvas bag and went outside.

Through the window of the newly built workshop, Walter could see his dad, Harry Speazlebud, working away on some new invention, happy as a swallow in flight. As Walter grabbed his bike his phone beeped. It was a text from his friend, Levon: 'Did u hear abt d asteroid? I bet dats wat killed d dinosaurs.'

Walter quickly texted him back: **'Hsibbur. Teb u ti t'nsaw.'**

Backwards spelling and talking was Walter's gift, and his appearances on TV had made him famous across the country. So it was easier for Walter to write backwards, and no problem for Levon – he had programmed a text-reverser into his phone to allow him to read Walter's texts easily.

Walter hopped on his bike and headed through the village to the community hall at the bottom of Nittiburg Hill. As he parked his bike against the wall his phone beeped once more.

'Betcha one euro.'

'Eruoy no!'

Walter changed into his kung-fu gear and

entered the room just as the class was beginning. At eleven years of age, his friend Annie Zuckers was by far the youngest kung-fu teacher in the country. She smiled as he entered, although she generally frowned upon lateness. She then joined her hands together, as if in prayer, and bowed to the class.

'Choose your partners, and assume combat positions,' she said calmly and gently. This always amazed Walter because he had seen the other Annie – the one you didn't want to mess with. She had called these two sides of her personality, 'Yin and Yang: the extremes that create the balance.' Walter didn't quite know what she was talking about, but he and Levon both loved saying the words 'Ying and Yang'. It sent them into convulsions of laughter.

When Walter finally woke up from his daydreaming all his possible partners had been snapped up.

'Guess it's you and me, cowboy,' said Annie, and the look in her eye said that today was not

Walter's lucky day. He swallowed hard and scrunched up his face, hoping his silent plea would find her mercy. Suddenly he felt the room rotate 360 degrees as gravity disappeared and, with a THUD!, he landed on his back on the soft mat.

Annie smiled down at him with her smoky blue eyes. 'Those who are not prepared are easy prey.'

Walter was feeling a little sore as he cycled home down Station Road, but his face glowed with happiness. Looking into Annie's eyes always had that effect on him, like eating Mrs Frost's NEW! Sherbet Lemon Zingers, or mango ice cream topped with Wilma Cartwright's whipped-cream fudge. He swung a right at the church on to Main Street, where he spotted Mrs Green polishing a pumpkin for her vegetable display.

'*Olleh, Retlaw,*' she called out.

'*Olleh Srm Neerg,*' he replied, chirpily. '*Sti a lufrednow yad.*'

But, as he crossed the river bridge on to

Sycamore Road, his smile began to fade. Then, as he slowed down and stopped outside St Anthony's graveyard, the smile vanished completely. Through the open gates, in the distance, he could see the tall, hand-carved headstone that marked his beloved grandad's grave. It had been almost a year now and Walter still had not made it through those gates. It was as if some invisible force field was holding him back – a force field of sadness.

Suddenly a man jumped out of a hole in the ground, giving Walter a fright. 'Oi! Master Speazlebud! I got one for ya today.' It was one-eyed Sam the gravedigger.

'Sam,' said Walter with a sigh of relief. 'You frightened the life out of me.'

'Sorry, mate,' said Sam as he ambled towards Walter, a cigarette dangling from his mouth. 'I spend 'alf me life diggin' 'oles and the other 'alf climbin outta them.' Sam had a London accent but nobody knew why – he had never been out of Nittiburg in his life.

Sam leaned up against the gatepost.

'Hippopotamus,' he said with a grin.

'*Sumatopoppih*,' replied Walter in a flash. 'Now I have one for you, Sam. "Dog".'

Sam had a good long think about it. 'G-O-D – God!'

'Excellent,' said Walter with a grin, 'but don't you think that if God knew his name backwards was dog, he would have called himself something else?'

'It's a wonder a'right. I never did think o' that before!'

Walter took a *Retlaw Dubelzaeps* backwards-spelling certificate from his bag – he never went anywhere without one – signed it and handed it to Sam.

Sam looked like he had just been given a million dollars. 'You should see your grandad's grave,' he said, his eyes still wide with gratitude. 'It's lookin' like a High King's garden for the anniversary next week. The geraniums and begonias and the roses are comin' along well.'

'Grandad loved roses,' said Walter.

'And where do you think I got the cuttings for my lovely roses? He gave them to me himself, he did. I reckon the day them roses bloom is the day you'll come through those gates, Master Speazlebud. I feel it in me bones, I do.'

Walter smiled. Grandad's anniversary would be a good day for him to finally pay his respects. He just didn't know if he would ever be brave enough to do it.

As soon as he arrived home, Walter turned on the brand-new computer, then opened Levon's email reverser, which allowed him to read his emails as quickly as anybody else. His mum was in India doing a yoga course and she emailed both Walter and his father Harry every day.

Today's email said: 'I have never felt so relaxed in all my life. I feel that nothing could disturb my inner peace,' and ended, 'See you next week. Love Mum.'

Walter's second email looked like junk mail but had mysteriously made it past Levon's 'junk mail' filter. It said: 'Global Emergency IMPORTANT.

US Gov.' Strangely, when Walter dragged it into the wastepaper basket, it bounced right out again.

He switched on his phone – Levon would know how to delete it. The phone beeped. His inbox said he had one voicemail. He pressed play.

A male voice with an American accent spoke slowly and clearly, 'Please check your email, Vice Commander Speazlebud. It contains urgent information.'

Walter raised an eyebrow. Only the National Aeronautical Space Authority (NASA) and the Central Bureau of Investigation (CIA) knew his official Apollo 11 mission title. He opened the email.

> *Dear Walter,*
>
> *It has been many years since your historic journey to the moon as Vice Commander of Apollo 11. History itself will forever be indebted to you for your heroic endeavours. Unfortunately an emergency of global importance has arisen and we feel you are our only hope. You will find attached an*

email booking for you and a guardian to
come to New York tomorrow morning to
discuss this urgent matter. I beg you to look
favourably upon our request.

Sincerely
John Hellerman
Head of Operations
CIA
PS. To prepare you for the meeting please
google 'Roswell 1947'.

Walter stared at the year 1947. Had the CIA got a time-travelling mission in mind? It caused his tummy muscles to tighten. Maybe he should just pretend that he had never opened the email.

There was a mechanical click, followed by a hum. The printer was printing out the email, but he hadn't pressed 'print'! It must be an automatic print-out mechanism programmed in by the CIA. He grabbed the print-out and headed for the kitchen.

As Walter poured himself a bowl of Choccopops, he heard his dad at the back door. *Good, he would soon help him make sense of the email.* He relaxed his tummy muscles and poured some milk into the bowl.

Harry Speazlebud came bumbling into the kitchen, his ragged red hair looking like it had been dipped in golden syrup and blow-dried by a turbo jet. He took his canvas bag of knick-knacks from his shoulder and put it on the ground.

'Nice bag, Dad', Walter said. 'I could do with one of those! Mine's full of holes. I lost one of my trainers on the way home.'

Harry appeared not to hear him and his scrunched-up brow told Walter there was something on his mind.

'Everything OK, Dad?'

'It might not be ready, Walt.'

'What might not be ready?'

'The world!'

'For what?' said Walter taking his bowl of Choccopops to the table and sitting down.

'My new invention.'

'What is it?'

Harry's puzzled expression suggested that this rather simple question was difficult for him to answer. 'It doesn't matter, Walt . . . according to the news, we're all about to be blown up . . . by an asteroid.'

Walter raised his eyes to heaven. 'Yeah, in a zillion years or something . . .'

Harry shook his head. 'Five hundred years, that's what they're saying.'

'Better run for cover then, Dad,' chuckled Walter. 'I'll dig the bunker if you nip to the shops for a thousand cans of beans.'

'Don't you care about the destruction of your lovely planet, Walt?' said Harry. 'If Hellvega doesn't annihilate the whole planet, it could still wipe out entire continents – many species of plants and animals will become extinct. Look at what happened to the dinosaurs!'

Walter dug his spoon into his cereal. 'There's absolutely no scientific proof that an asteroid killed all the dinosaurs. They could have simply evolved into birds! You should know that. You're a scientist.'

'Inventor, actually.'

'You're a scientist who invents, then!'

'I'm an inventor who . . . whatever . . . Is something wrong, Walt?'

'What do you mean?'

'It's your voice . . . if it was a bird it would be flying crooked.' Harry was quick like that. He could read Walter's moods as if they were written across his forehead in Day-Glo lettering.

'I've just got an email from the CIA.'

'I knew it,' said Harry with a wicked smile. 'They're on your tail. They've heard you're a serial killer!'

'I'm a whaaaaaat?'

'A cereal killer. There's not a day goes by you don't murder a bowl of those Choccopops!'

'Ha, ha,' said Walter, handing Harry the print-out.

As Harry read the email his left eyebrow

began to rise like the eyebrow of a ventriloquist's dummy. 'An "emergency of global importance"! Hmm. Intriguing. Hmm. Fascinating.' He read to the end of the email. '"Roswell 1947". Roswell was where one of the most talked-about alien sightings *ever* took place, Walt! Let's hit the "Big Apple" and find out what it's all about!'

Walter shrugged his shoulders.

'How can you say no to an offer like this? It could be an adventure.'

'You can go. Tell them I'm afraid of flying.'

'They know you flew to the moon in 1969! You weren't afraid then.'

'People change.'

Harry put his hand on his son's shoulder. 'They do, Walt – people like Granduncle Bob, whose life was changed for the better by you travelling back in time.'

Walter had never thought of it like that but he was glad that Bob no longer had to carry a lie around inside him.

'*And* you were the first person on the moon,

Walt!' continued Harry. 'You're brave, you're adventurous! You've got to throw yourself back into life again.'

Walter jumped up from the table. 'I went back in time for Grandad, but he's not around any more!' He grabbed the email, ran out through the kitchen door and up the stairs.

Walter lay on his bed staring at the plastic stars on the ceiling and wiping a tear from his eye. How he wished his grandad was here right now. He closed his eyes and tried to imagine him singing 'Danny Boy' backwards, like he used to do every night before he went to sleep, but it was no use, he couldn't make the sound of Grandad's voice come alive in his mind. He glanced at the email on the bedside table. Imagine if Grandad could send him an email, or a sign, just to let him know he was out there somewhere, that he had not gone completely from his life. Just then he felt a strange sensation that sent a tingle up his spine. It was as if an invisible cloud had brushed his skin. Then he noticed something shimmering in his peripheral vision. He glanced across at the email on the table again. The words 'you are our only hope' glowed, as if they had just caught the rays of an invisible sun. Then he heard the voice of Grandad from deep inside his mind, so clear that Grandad could have been in the room beside him. 'Be brave, Walter, be brave.'

Later that evening, Walter heard a knock on the door.

'Come in.'

When Harry entered the room he found Walter looking through his telescope. 'I haven't seen you use your telescope in a year,' said Harry.

'Take a look, Dad. It's a new moon.'

Harry put his eye to the eyepiece. 'You were there, Walt. You landed on the moon; you walked on its surface.'

Walter smiled. 'Sorry for storming out . . .' he said.

Harry smiled and placed his hand on

Walter's shoulder. 'Is no your final decision, Vice Commander Speazlebud? There's a Leonardo da Vinci exhibition at the New York Metropolitan Museum of Art, you know.'

Walter glanced at the email sitting on the bedside table. 'Do you think they want us to go all the way to New York to talk about *aliens*?' he asked.

'Don't you believe in them?'

Walter hesitated a moment. 'I know Grandad did but I'm not sure . . . then when I was on the moon I saw a bright light jumping about in the distance. On the way back to earth I asked Commander Armstrong what it was and he said, "Aliens, probably. Every astronaut sees them."'

'So you'll go?' Harry asked.

'What would Mum say?'

'She's nervous about time travelling, but she loves New York.'

Walter stared at the wall. 'Annie's been on the subway. She saw rats as big as lambs!'

'Sure, but they're hard to catch. We may

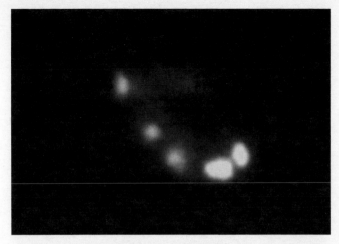

The strange bright lights spotted by the crew of the Apollo 11 mission.

have to settle for pizza! Besides, I'm vegetarian,' Harry joked.

'I hate rats,' protested Walter as he looked out of the window at the moon.

'A new moon,' said Harry, following Walter's gaze. 'Your grandad said that the new moon was a good time to start an adventure.'

'It is,' said Walter.

'Is that a yes, then?'

Walter looked at Harry as a smile brightened

his face. 'If I'm going to New York I'll need a new canvas bag with a secret pocket for the Giftstone!'

Harry took twenty euros from his pocket. 'You pop down in the morning and get yourself one. I'll email Mum to tell her about our plans.'

Na Reffo eh nac Esufer

Walter looked out through the window at the glistening Atlantic Ocean as, beside him, Harry nodded off to sleep. He thought about the email from the CIA and it made him nervous, especially now that he had accepted the invitation. Maybe it was the words 'emergency of global importance' or the word 'alien' – things he didn't quite understand often had this effect on him.

He reached down and took his brand-new canvas bag from beneath the seat, opened it and removed the small box containing the Ruby Giftstone from the concealed pouch inside the flap. He opened the box, removed the Giftstone and rolled it around in his hand. It comforted him to feel its smooth surface, though he sensed that the days ahead might not be quite so smooth. He returned the Giftstone to the pouch then he, too, fell asleep.

A chisel-faced police officer greeted Walter and Harry as they stepped from the plane at JFK International Airport.

'Officer Shelley,' he said as he reached out his hand in greeting. 'Welcome to New York.'

With Officer Shelley leading the way, Walter and Harry picked up their cases, then walked out into the New York sunshine.

'It's hot,' said Walter, wiping the perspiration from his brow while opening his shirt an extra button.

'Eighty-six degrees with ninety-six per cent humidity, at a guess,' said Harry.

'That's what I said,' said Walter. 'It's hot!'

Officer Shelley walked across the pick-up area towards a smiling grey-haired black man who was holding open the back door of a limousine.

Walter said 'Hi,' jumped in the back, sank into the soft leather seats and closed his eyes. 'That's more like it,' he said as cool air blew from a directional jet above his head.

'Turbo Macro-zoom Liquid-chilled remote conditioning!' said Harry excitedly as he sat beside him. 'That'll cool you down, Walt.'

'Right on,' replied the driver. 'How did ya guess it was Turbo Macro-zoom?'

'Because . . . I . . . I invented it,' said Harry, slightly embarrassed.

The driver and police officer glanced in the rear-view mirror. 'You did?' they said in unison, but Harry said no more.

This didn't surprise Walter – his dad had become hugely successful ever since NASA used his suspension system for the moon buggy, but his success had hardly affected him.

'You do know that the United Nations Assembly is being held in your hotel this week?' said Officer Shelley as they turned on to the freeway.

'Yep,' said Harry. 'They couldn't have picked a busier week to have us over!'

'What's the United Nations Assembly?' asked Walter.

'It's where the world's leaders get together

and tackle the big problems,' said Harry.

'Emergencies of global importance?' said Walter with a nervous smile.

'Exactly,' said Harry. 'I guess that's why they want us here.'

They took the Queensboro Bridge to New York's most famous borough – Manhattan – and on first glimpse the city, full of mystery, beauty and promise, captured Walter's heart. As a traffic jam on the bridge caused the limousine to slow to a halt, Walter used his camera phone to take photographs of the Manhattan skyline.

'You're the regular tourist,' said Harry, 'snap, snap, snap.'

'It's for Levon and Annie. I texted them to say we were going away but I didn't say where. I'll send the pictures over the phone.'

'Annie will be over on the next plane,' said Harry teasingly.

Walter gave his dad a good dig in the ribs.

'She went back to 1969 with you,' said Harry, 'didn't she?'

'That was an accident,' said Walter. 'Grandad got the **Noitanigami** spell wrong.'

'Oh, of course,' said Harry. 'He wasn't well, was he?' Walter noticed a hint of sadness in Harry's eyes. Sometimes it was easy for Walter to forget that Harry missed him too, that Walter's grandad had also been Harry's dad. He put his hand on his dad's arm and squeezed it gently.

As the traffic began to move again, Walter wrote a text to accompany the photographs. Levon's read, '**ahcteb a hsifdlog uoy t'nod wonk tahw ytic m'I ni**.'

And to Annie, he texted, '**Ni Wen Kroy. Ycnegreme gniteem. Gnihtyna dluoc neppah**.'

That'll put a smile on her face, he thought. Annie loved New York – she visited the city every year with her parents – and she loved adventure.

'Should I send one to Mum in India?' said Walter to Harry.

'Let's see how she responds to the email first,' said Harry. 'We don't want to upset her inner peace!'

The limousine exited the bridge on to 59th Street, travelled downtown to 50th Street, crossed the avenues and swung a left on to Park Avenue, eventually pulling up outside the Waldorf Astoria Hotel.

'One of the most famous hotels in the world,' said the driver. 'I hope you enjoy your stay.'

A small freckled man with bushy red eyebrows and a green uniform appeared at the curb side and opened the door. 'Mister and Master Speazlebud, is it yerselves?' he said. 'Pat Finnegan, hotel concierge, at your service!'

Harry and Walter climbed out of the limo and shook Finnegan's hand. The pavement felt soft beneath Walter's feet. He looked down. He was standing on a red carpet that ran from the sidewalk to the revolving brass doors of the hotel.

'You're both Irish!' said Finnegan. 'I can tell by the twinkle in yer eyes!'

Walter nodded, then wiped the sweat from his brow.

'Feelin' the heat?' said Finnegan. 'I'm here

forty years and I'm still not used to it. You could fry an egg on the sidewalk.' Then he pointed to the flags of the world suspended above the doorway. 'Heads of state from all over the world are staying here right now as well as rock stars, Hollywood actors and millionaires.'

'I'm surprised there was room for us!' said Harry, while helping Finnegan to put the bags on a trolley.

'There wasn't,' replied Finnegan. 'We had to move a Greek tycoon and his son so that ye could have the Panoramic suite. He wasn't too happy, I can tell ya! He was rantin' and ravin'!'

Walter blushed. At moments like this he always felt like hiding.

Walter and Harry followed Finnegan through the revolving door and up the marble steps. A glamorously dressed couple threw Walter and Harry a dirty glance.

'I guess they think we're a little under-dressed,' said Harry to Finnegan.

'Jeans and t-shirts is grand when yer really

important,' said Finnegan, 'it's when yer not that ya have to dress up!'

They crossed the mosaicked marbled foyer where Finnegan stopped beneath a huge crystal chandelier. 'It's been in lots of movies,' said Finnegan.

'I saw it in *The Pink Panther*,' said Walter.

Finnegan nodded. 'Some people say that the moment ya pass under that chandelier your life becomes like a movie. So be prepared for adventure!'

'I like movies,' said Walter, 'and I like adventure, but I also like happy endings.'

'And as me dear oul grandmother used to say,' said Finnegan, 'what's for ya won't go by ya.'

'Grandad used to say that too,' said Walter.

'So you know what it means?'

'Not really.'

'It means that if it's time for you to have an adventure you'll have an adventure!'

The elevator journey to the fortieth floor was a slow one as they stopped to allow guests on and off, so Walter decided to check his messages.

'Ur in Nu Yok, and u o me a gldfsh,' said Levon, while Annie's response read, 'Where u stayin?'

'*Frodlaw Letoh*,' replied Walter. '*Hteitrof roolf*!'

'This is your stop,' said Finnegan as the elevator door opened.

They crossed the hallway to a door which said 'Panoramic suite'. Finnegan opened the door then stood back and gestured for his guests to step inside.

Walter felt like he had just stumbled into a palace drawing room – hand-carved antique furniture sat on a deep-piled carpet, an engraved silver-framed mirror hung over a marbled fireplace and woven silk ropes tied up crimson window drapes.

'Just like home!' said Harry, putting his shoulder bag on the ground and stretching out on the chaise longue.

Finnegan removed a small, battered, gnome-like metal figurine from his pocket and placed it on the mantelpiece. 'Twill keep yis both safe and sound.'

Finnegan turned to Harry and held his hand out for a tip. Harry opened his wallet and removed a crisp five-dollar bill, but Finnegan's disappointed expression clearly indicated that a little more would be appreciated. Harry handed him another dollar. 'God bless yis both,' said Finnegan with a wink. 'I'm trying to raise a few shillings to go home to see me mother.' With that he scuttled out the door.

'Strange little man,' said Harry.

'Levon would say he's "a bit shifty",' said Walter, then he walked across the room, slid open the glass door, stepped on to the balcony and pulled the door closed behind him. What a view! He was surrounded by the landmarks of New York – the Chrysler building with its star-shaped crown to the east, the Empire State to the south, and, across the river, in the distance, just visible through the fog rising from the Hudson River, the Statue of Liberty, her torch held high to light the immigrants' way.

Just then, something caught Walter's eye – a man wearing dark glasses standing on a hotel balcony directly across the street talking into a cell phone. *Probably just security*, thought Walter.

'Walter!' It was Harry calling from the living room.

Through the glass doors, Walter could see a tall, grey-haired man and a small, thin, blonde-haired woman talking to Harry. They were both immaculately dressed and their demeanour suggested that they meant business. Walter took a deep breath, pulled back the glass doors, and stepped into the room.

'Aha, Walter Speazlebud,' said the tall man, reaching out his hand in greeting. His handshake was firm and his voice deep and confident. 'What a pleasure to meet one of the most important people in history,' he said with a gracious smile. 'I'm John Hellerman, Head of Operations, CIA.'

'What does that mean?' said Walter.

'It means that I am charged by the Central Investigation Agency with the planning and execution of all major intelligence operations.'

'Execution?' said Walter.

'It means "carrying out",' said Harry. 'Nobody's going to die!'

'I don't want to be carried out either!' said Walter with a laugh, but Hellerman didn't smile.

'We hope nobody is going to die,' he said, then he gestured to the lady standing by his side. 'Miss Veronica Casserina, US Secretary of State.'

'Nice to meet you, Walter,' the lady said. 'I've heard so much about you.'

Walter recognised her. He had seen her on the news and sitting in the front row at Wrestlemania.

'The President had hoped to attend our meeting,' she said. 'Unfortunately, he is tied up with the United Nations Assembly downstairs. I will brief him as soon as our meeting is over.'

This sounded serious! What had Walter let himself in for?

Hellerman pulled up an armchair for Secretary Casserina and gestured for Walter and

Harry to sit opposite her. He then removed a laptop computer from his briefcase and placed it on the table in the centre of the room.

'A lucky leprechaun!' said Casserina, noticing the figurine on the mantlepiece. 'How cute.'

Hellerman switched on his laptop and turned to Walter. 'I'm sure you would like to know why Secretary Casserina and I have brought you here?'

Walter nodded.

'What do you know about Roswell?'

'Dad told me it's where an alien spaceship crashed ages ago so I looked it up on the internet. A lot of experts think that the story was made up.'

Hellerman folded his arms and his expression showed that he did not like being doubted. 'On 2nd July 1947, a couple heard a crash in the desert. When they investigated, they found what looked like the wreckage of a flying saucer. They called the military. A few days later the government issued a statement that said the remains of a UFO had been found.'

Walter said nothing. It was one thing thinking that aliens may exist but it was a different thing when somebody was looking you in the eye and asking you to believe it.

Secretary Casserina took up the story. 'Many people believe that the statement made by the government was to cover up the fact that the military were testing a nuclear bomb and needed to seal the area off.' She paused, then continued, 'There was a cover-up. The army *was* testing nuclear missiles at our military site in Roswell. But . . . there *were* aliens!' She nodded to Hellerman, who continued, 'During the testing of a nuclear missile, two of them were accidentally killed.'

'Two of what?' said Walter, still finding it difficult to let go of his doubt.

'Two alien beings from Assina, a planet orbiting the giant red star Betelgeuse, in the constellation of Orion.'

Walter looked at Harry to see his reaction to what Hellerman was saying, but Harry's eyes were closed in concentration.

The front page of the Roswell Daily News following
the capture of the Assinian spaceship in 1947.

'They had left their spaceship,' continued
Hellerman, 'and were walking across the desert
towards the control tower when the bomb went off.'

Harry's eyes opened and his jaw dropped,
while Walter's face remained expressionless.

'It was a tragedy, and a terrible loss,' said
Secretary Casserina, placing the palms of her
hands together as if in prayer. 'These aliens had
been protecting the earth for thousands of years.'

'Why would they want to protect us?' said
Harry, looking at her, his expression full of
childlike wonder.

'We were a beautiful discovery to the
Assinians,' she continued. 'They were enthralled
by us. They called our planet their "Curious

Flower", and to ensure our survival they destroyed any asteroid that threatened us.'

'Hmm,' said Harry, rubbing his chin. 'I had often wondered why the moon was peppered with asteroid craters while the earth seemed to get off lightly. How did they do it?'

'We have been told that they used a "mass displacement inversion device" powered by dark energy from a black hole,' said Hellerman.

'I knew that those black holes would be useful for something!' said Harry. 'I've been studying them for years.'

'Then we discovered nuclear power . . . and WE became a threat.'

'To the Assinian aliens?' said Harry.

'No,' said Secretary Casserina, 'to ourselves.' Walter and Harry shifted their gaze in her direction. 'The aliens tried to make contact with various government sources during the 1940s, using coded radio signals, but those who acted on this information and tried to convince the president were not believed.'

'Then the aliens landed,' said Hellerman. He paused, as if for dramatic effect. 'And they got blown up.'

'But they only wanted to save us from ourselves!' said Walter, being drawn into the story like a fish on a line.

Hellerman and Secretary Casserina both nodded in agreement.

'Did they find alien bodies?' asked Harry. 'I saw some photographs on the internet but I couldn't tell if they were real or not.'

'No, the aliens outside were vaporised,' said Hellerman. 'Those fake alien bodies were used to distract the media from what had really happened.'

'And the spaceship?' said Walter.

Hellerman shook his head. 'It was unharmed. It had a shield that protected it from both the radiation and the shock waves of the blast. It's not possible to navigate through deep space without such protection.'

'Even if what you are saying is true,' said

Harry, 'what has it got to do with Walter?'

Hellerman didn't respond. He just took a disc from his briefcase, placed it in the DVD player of his laptop and clicked on 'play'. A bright flickering light moved slowly across the screen. 'This is Hellvega, as viewed through NASA's Astralgazer Superzoom telescope,' Hellerman said. 'This asteroid is big enough to wipe out North America. The tsunami that will inevitably follow will flood the entire earth within days. All living species will be eliminated, including mankind. There will be no survivors.'

'It probably won't get within a million miles of the earth,' said Walter. 'They seldom do.'

Hellerman minimised the image and switched to a live video feed of a thin, nervous-looking old man with gold-rimmed glasses and white bushy eyebrows.

'That's Rolf Hardy, the famous astro-physicist,' whispered Harry excitedly to Walter.

'Step over here please, Walter,' said Hellerman, 'and face the built-in webcam.'

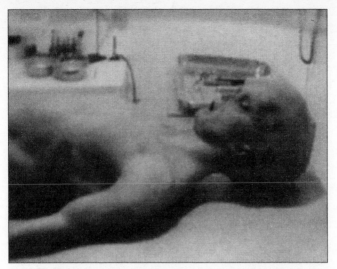

This fake alien autopsy uses a plastic alien modelled on the captured Assinian alien Zenon (AI).

Walter stood up and stood in the spot indicated by Hellerman.

'Dr Hardy, I would like you to meet Mr Walter Speazlebud, Vice Commander of Apollo 11 and first person on the moon.'

The doctor clasped his hands together and bowed to the camera.

'Dr Hardy specialises in the study of asteroids, Walter. He will now explain his startling discovery.'

Dr Hardy unclasped his hands. 'I originally discovered Hellvega over ten years ago, but its recent, sudden change of course defies all scientific explanation. By our calculations, it will hit the earth within . . .' he paused, 'five days.'

'FIVE DAYS?' said Harry. 'The radio said five hundred years!'

'We didn't want to cause worldwide panic' said Hellerman. 'Have you any questions, Walter?'

'No,' said Walter, shaking his head in disbelief.

Harry sat up straight, a look of deep concern informing his expression. 'I would like to ask Dr Hardy one question,' he said.

'Feel free,' said Hellerman, gesturing for Harry to step towards the laptop.

'Dr Hardy,' said Harry, 'I would like to know how an asteroid can suddenly change course like this?'

We believe that the scientists of the planet Assina used their "mass displacement inversion device" to alter the asteroid's course, and sent it on a path directly towards earth,' the doctor replied.

Walter held his head with his hands as if he was attempting to stop his brain from exploding. He looked up at Hellerman.

'But you said that the aliens saved our planet by *blowing up* asteroids!'

'That's true,' said Hellerman, 'until we killed two of their citizens – the First Contact Ambassador and his wife.'

'But why wait until now to look for revenge?' said Harry.

'This is not revenge; this is blackmail!' said Secretary Casserina, jumping up from her chair as if she had just been bitten on the backside by a sharp-toothed insect. 'The Assinians want their people back, alive, or the earth will be destroyed.'

'But their people have been dead since 1947,' said Harry.

Hellerman grimaced, placed both hands on Walter's shoulders and looked him in the eye. 'That's where you come in, Walter. The Assinians want you to go back to 1947 and warn the aliens, giving them a chance to return to their spaceship and leave the danger area before the bomb explodes. Walter, listen carefully, the world is under extreme threat and YOU are the only person who can save it.'

'Aren't there other p-people who can t-time t-travel?' stuttered Walter.

'Sure,' said Secretary Casserina, 'there are lots of charlatans, quacks and conmen who claim to have your powers but none we could trust and none who possesses your bravery. But you must be under no illusions: this mission is extremely dangerous.'

'There's just a three-minute window,' said Hellerman.

Walter suddenly felt faint. 'A three-minute window?'

'There were two minutes and fifty-nine seconds exactly between the time the aliens left the spaceship and the exact moment the bomb exploded,' said Secretary Casserina.

'Then *boom*?' said Walter.

'I wouldn't put it so dramatically . . .' said Hellerman.

Harry lay down on the chaise longue and closed his eyes – the paleness of his face contrasted with the deep crimson of the upholstery.

Secretary Casserina placed her hand gently on Walter's shoulder. 'You enabled Man to go to the moon, Walter. Will you also be the one to save the earth?'

Harry suddenly jumped to his feet. 'There is a way that we can destroy or divert the asteroid.'

'Sure,' said Hellerman, 'if we can figure out how the Assinians' "mass displacement inversion" technology works.'

'Exactly,' said Harry.

Dr Hardy shifted restlessly onscreen. 'We have had a team of scientists working on it for years. It's beyond our current scientific understanding.'

'But maybe I could help you in your research,' said Harry. 'I've been studying black holes –'

'We must keep our attention focused on the most effective plan,' interrupted Secretary Casserina.

'Surely it's worth a try,' pleaded Harry. 'The future of the earth is at stake!'

Secretary Casserina responded with anger in her voice. 'With all due respect, Mr Speazlebud, it is highly unlikely that you will be able to solve a problem that has baffled our scientists for so long. Subject closed!'

Harry flopped back down on to the chaise longue.

Secretary Casserina turned her attention to Walter. 'What is your answer, Walter?'

Walter looked away to avoid her stare. 'I've got five days to think about it,' he said.

'I'm afraid not,' said Hellerman. 'While we have told the press the asteroid will hit in five hundred years, the real information has been leaked to some high-powered business people, causing oil prices to rise and stock-exchange share prices to plummet. We reckon that we have just one day before the truth spreads and society begins to break down.'

Walter felt his legs tremble and panic tighten his tummy muscles. Even if he saved the world he would still be risking his own life! 'I-I'm not s-sure about this,' he stuttered.

Secretary Casserina leaned over and whispered something in Hellerman's ear. He nodded, said goodbye to Dr Hardy, and brought up an image of what looked like a bald man sitting in the corner of a small prison cell, his head resting in his gloved hands. Hellerman spoke clearly into the microphone, 'Al, remove your hands from your head and face the camera.'

Al raised his head from his hands and looked directly at the camera. His eyes blinked, as if he had just woken up.

An 'Aaahh' sound came from Walter's mouth, which clearly expressed his shock and fear, then he grabbed the back of an armchair with both hands to steady himself. It was weird staring at something you never really believed existed.

Hellerman pressed 'zoom' and the camera closed in to reveal Al's oversized head and orange-tinged oval eyes, his small mouth and pointed ears.

'Al has been with us since 1947,' said Hellerman.

'Who is he?' asked Harry, standing up, his expression one of both excitement and curiosity.

'He was the pilot of the Assinian spaceship that landed in Roswell. An aeronautical engineer and designer by profession, he was a huge loss to his planet's space travel and surveillance programme – and a big help to ours. He provided the knowledge and expertise that allowed NASA to develop its space programme. Without him, neither your son nor any other astronaut would have landed on the moon.'

'Miss O'Connor never told us that in school!' Walter exclaimed.

'To quote a great man,' replied Secretary Casserina, '"Secrecy is essential in all the affairs of the state".' She coughed, then continued, 'Al was inside the spaceship when the accident, to which Mr Hellerman has referred, happened. He was knocked unconscious by the force of the blast but the shock-wave protection built into the UFO's surface metal meant that the craft remained intact and Al was shaken but unharmed. Since being captured, he has enjoyed a good life, living in underground luxury at our military base in New Mexico with generous perks and relative freedom.'

'Freedom?' said Walter. 'But he's in jail!'

'He was moved to the high-security lock-up wing three days ago,' said Hellerman gently, in an attempt to calm Walter down, 'when his people threatened to annihilate the world. He *was* "one of us". Now he's an enemy – he has sided with his world against ours.'

'How does he communicate with his people?' asked Harry, his voice charged with excitement.

'Telepathically it seems. He foretold the exact time and date the asteroid would change course.'

Hellerman closed down the video feed and

turned off the computer. 'The President will address the United Nations Assembly in the ballroom of the hotel in the morning. This issue is, of course, number one on our agenda. What's your decision, Walter?'

'I . . . I need time to think about it,' Walter replied.

Secretary Casserina smiled as she turned to Harry. 'Mr Hellerman and I trust that you will permit your son to carry out his mission if his answer is yes?'

'I . . . know his grandad is watching over him . . . but I would be lying if I said I wouldn't be worried,' Harry said.

'Will you allow him to go if his answer is yes?' said Hellerman sharply.

'I'll support whatever decision Walter makes,' said Harry.

Secretary Casserina and Hellerman seemed satisfied with Harry's response.

'I just need some time to think about it,' repeated Walter.

'That's all that we ask,' said Hellerman, 'but time is ticking on.'

A Tahc Htiw eht Neila

Walter barely said a word during dinner with Harry while the waiting staff fussed over them like royalty. There wasn't much to say, just a big decision to be made. When they returned upstairs Walter said goodnight then went to the balcony to watch the sun set over the city. He wished that Grandad's voice might appear in his mind to guide him, but no words appeared, or if they did, they must have been drowned out by the sounds of the city – the screaming of ambulances, the honking of horns, the hum of air conditioners! From the corner of his eye he spotted the man he had seen yesterday on the balcony across the street.

That night, for the first time in over a year, Walter did not dream that he was floating in space while the world drifted away from him. Instead, he dreamed of asteroids bombarding the earth and Al the alien floating around his prison cell like an astronaut in space repeating Neil Armstrong's famous words, 'This is one small step for Man, one giant leap for mankind.'

Harry was sitting at the table when Walter shuffled into the sitting room at 7.30 a.m. the next morning. 'You're up early, Walter. Sleep well?'

Walter shook his head.

'Me neither,' said Harry, holding his notepad in the air. 'I've been trying to figure out how the aliens' "mass displacement inversion device" works so you won't have to go back in time. Not making much progress though.'

'Dad,' said Walter, pouring himself a glass of orange juice from the lavish breakfast spread that had been laid out for them, 'do you believe that Al the alien was really the brains behind the Apollo 11 space mission?'

'Sure,' said Harry. 'An engineer capable of designing a spaceship that could travel from the star Betelgeuse to earth, which is 425 light years away, would regard sending a rocket to the moon, which is only about 250 thousand miles away, as mere child's play.'

Walter nodded, then he glanced at the two morning newspapers lying side by side on the table.

'Dramatic slump in world economy,' said the *Daily Standard*.

'World under threat,' said the *New York Times*.

'Nothing like a bit of good news to cheer a body up,' said Harry sarcastically. 'Seems like Hellerman was right.'

Walter nodded, then turned on his mobile phone. It beeped twice. He had texted Levon and Annie before going to sleep last night and updated them on his news. Levon's reply said, 'Always wnted 2b abdcted by n alien,' but Annie's was more helpful: 'Everybody knows that aliens don't exist, but if d survival of d human race depends on it it might b worth believing.'

Before Walter had a chance to reply, his phone rang.

It was John Hellerman. 'What's your decision, Walter?'

'I want to meet the alien,' said Walter.

'Walter, there are FOUR days left before the asteroid makes contact with the earth . . . The world's economy is sliding by the hour . . . and you want to go on a day trip to New Mexico?'

'I need to meet the alien,' repeated Walter, 'then I'll decide.'

'Hold the line,' said Hellerman frostily. He was back within seconds. 'A car will pick you up in an hour. You must come alone.' Then Hellerman hung up.

'You want to meet the alien before you decide,' said Harry. 'Can't argue with that, Walt.'

'You don't mind me going there alone?' Walter asked his dad.

'You went back to 1969 on your own, Walt. You can do a day trip to New Mexico! I'm off to the da Vinci exhibition.'

Walter gave Harry a high five. 'See you this evening, Dad.'

A four-seater Albatros jet took Walter from the

military wing of JFK airport to the Roswell military base in New Mexico – a journey of 2,500 miles – in under three hours. Walter stepped from the plane on to the hot tarmac and looked around; he was in the centre of a tower-guarded desert fortress surrounded by an electric fence topped with razor wire. He squinted in the sunshine as a rotund young woman with a shaved head and wearing army fatigues walked towards him through the haze.

'I'm General Hopkins,' she said in a Southern drawl, reaching out her hand in greeting. 'Mighty pleased to meet you, Walter.'

'I'm pleased to meet you too, General,' replied Walter.

'Hope you got some sun protector on,' said Hopkins with an air of genuine concern. 'Red hair, pale skin, you'll burn up if you don't.'

Walter nodded. Harry had made sure he had packed his factor 50 before he left.

'Don't suppose you've ever spoken to an alien before?' she said as she led Walter to her old, open-top army jeep.

'Never,' said Walter. 'What's he like?'

'If he hadn't turned traitor, I'd say he was a nice guy, but we've had to show him that any threat against our nation, against the world, cannot and will not be tolerated. That's why he's in prison right now.'

'But your atomic-testing unit accidentally killed the First Contact Ambassador of his planet and his wife.'

Hopkins cleared her throat.

'You mean his dad and his mom?'

'Hellerman never told me that!' said Walter.

'He reckoned he had told you enough for one day, Walter. Al was their only son – the apple of their eye. He loved them too and, even though he didn't plan this attack, he hasn't told his Assinian friends to call it off.'

'Because he wants to see his parents again,' said Walter.

'You got it,' said Hopkins, 'but it still makes him an accomplice.'

Hopkins opened the passenger door of her

jeep and Walter jumped in. With red-tail eagles circling above them, they drove across the hot desert sands to the door of a heavily guarded, bunker-like building.

'This is where we keep our special prisoners,' said Hopkins, climbing out of the jeep. 'Nobody has ever escaped from here. Nobody has ever even tried.' Her words sent a shiver down Walter's spine.

An armed officer escorted Walter and Hopkins into the building, through a series of long corridors, separated by metal doors, until they reached cell number 399. The officer unlocked the door and stepped aside.

'Are you ready?' said Hopkins.

Walter bit his lip, then nodded.

Hopkins stepped into the cell and Walter followed. A tiny window leaked a beam of sunshine that illuminated the bald, gloved figure sitting on a wooden chair with his head in his hands. Behind Walter, the metal door went CLANG!

'Show us your face, Al,' said Hopkins in a voice neither hostile nor gentle.

Al uncovered his face, and sat up straight. Walter took a step backwards. Al's head seemed larger, and his orange eyes brighter than they had appeared on the screen of Hellerman's laptop. His skin had a soft orange tinge, too. Al smiled. It was a warm and welcoming smile. Walter smiled back – he couldn't help himself – Al's smile was one of the most beautiful smiles he had ever seen, but it wasn't just his smile that affected Walter, it was the sense of joy that radiated from every cell in Al's body. This really was an alien being, a very special alien being.

'Remove your gloves, Al,' instructed Hopkins with a smirk. 'Just in case Walter's not convinced you're an alien!'

'There's no need . . .' said Walter.

'Take them off anyway,' ordered Hopkins, 'just for fun.'

Al removed his gloves and dropped them on to the floor, one by one. His hands were extraordinary – each one had three long, slender fingers and one small thumb.

Walter opened his mouth to say something and a 'Levonism' popped out, 'Wicked.'

'I take it that you have used a modern expression to infer your understandable incredulity?' said Al. His voice was clear and strong and his diction perfect.

Walter chuckled. He hadn't a clue what Al meant.

Hopkins leaned towards him and whispered in his ear. 'Don't be drawn in by his charm, Walter.'

'"I cannot hide what I am",' said the alien.

'It's a quote from Shakespeare,' said Hopkins, throwing her eyes to heaven.

'*King Lear*, to be precise,' Al replied with a smile.

Walter looked puzzled. 'You speak English like a British person!'

'We Assinians have acquired the basics of all earthly languages,' Al replied. 'However, my English was enormously improved with the help of an Oxford professor, an American spy given a safe haven by the CIA.'

'Enough of your life story already,' snapped Hopkins. 'We've got more important things to talk about today.'

The alien turned to Walter. 'My given name is Zenon, but you can call me Al if you wish. Everybody else does.'

'I'm Walter.'

'I know, dear boy,' said the alien, clasping his hands together. 'Your first step on the moon was the proudest moment of my brief time here on earth – the end result of twenty-two years' work with my team of NASA scientists.'

'I couldn't have done it without you, could I?' asked Walter. 'Your expertise allowed NASA to build the rocket that took us to the moon.'

'And we couldn't have done it without you,' said Al. 'Your bravery made it possible.'

'What's this?' barked Hopkins. 'The alien–earthling mutual appreciation society?'

Walter ignored Hopkins and stared in silence

at the alien as memories of his moon journey came flooding back.

'"I like your silence",' said Al, '"it the more shows off your wonder".'

'Erm, *Hamlet*?' said Walter, taking a wild guess.

'Yes! Wonderful!' replied Al. 'Are you a fan of the Bard?'

Walter shook his head. 'My grandad was, though, and he often read me bits from Shakespeare's plays.'

'You said your grandad "was". Can I respectfully ask, did he fall out of love with the great Bard's works or has he shuffled off this mortal coil, as you humans say? Did he . . . die, Walter?'

'Yes, he . . . died,' said Walter, tears instantly welling up in his eyes. He had never said those words before. 'It's his anniversary in six days' time. It'll be one year.'

Al looked at Walter with compassion in his orange eyes. 'Our bloods may differ, but we are tied together in loss.'

'*Romeo and Juliet*?' said Walter, taking another wild guess.

'No,' replied Al, a gentle smile stretching his lips. 'I made that one up myself.'

The tears of sadness that sat in the corners of Walter's eyes slowly turned to tears of laughter, as if they had been touched by the magic of alchemy. And once he started laughing, he just couldn't stop himself.

'It wasn't that funny, Walter!' shouted Hopkins. 'Remember, he is not your friend. He is threatening to destroy the world!'

Al's eyes seemed to widen and brighten simultaneously. 'My people have waited for many years for my parents to be returned to them, just as I have done, but if you decide not to go I shall bear you no ill.'

'If he decides not to go we all get blown up,' screamed Hopkins.

'Not if somebody here on earth discovers how our mass displacement diversion technology works,' said Al with a gentle smile.

'My dad's trying to work it out,' said Walter, 'but he's not making much progress.'

'I was most impressed by the suspension system he created for the moon buggy,' said Al. 'I hadn't thought of it myself! If anyone could crack it, Harry can.'

Hopkins placed her hand on Walter's shoulder and yanked him physically in the direction of the door. 'Let's go. NOW!'

As the cell door clanged shut behind them, Hopkins said, 'If you decide not to go, the world will end in four days. There are no other options!'

'If I go back in time,' replied Walter firmly, 'it will be for my own reasons and not for yours, Hellerman's or Secretary Casserina's.'

Hopkins stared at him, her eyes full of fire. She wasn't used to being spoken to like that. Walter didn't flinch – instead he continued to hold her gaze, because deep down he knew he was the one in charge. Hopkins eventually turned her gaze away and shouted, 'Let's go!'

As Walter was led back through corridor

after corridor, Al's voice echoed in his head. 'Our bloods may differ, but we are tied together in loss.'

The moment Walter stepped outside the prison and into the New Mexico sunshine he switched on his phone, located speed dial, selected the number and pressed 'dial'. 'Mr Hellerman,' he said calmly and with confidence, 'I have made my decision . . .'

'Grand day,' said Finnegan, opening the door of Walter's limousine.

'It is,' replied Walter. And he meant it. He had made his decision. He had agreed to travel back in time the next morning, after a good night's sleep. It surprised him that, instead of feeling nervous, he wanted to jump up in the air and click his heels! He couldn't wait to tell Harry.

'Have you seen my dad?' he asked Finnegan.

'I sent him off to the art museum in a taxi at ten o'clock this morning and I haven't laid eyes on him since,' Finnegan replied.

Walter looked at his watch. It was 5.45 p.m.

'Ah, Walter, you're back.'

He looked up. Hellerman was walking towards him across the hotel lobby. He placed his hand on Walter's shoulder and whispered, 'Because of what you have agreed to do the

General Assembly has arranged to sit late in the ballroom this evening. They would like to meet you before you commence your mission.'

'Why?' said Walter.

'Because the world you are about to save wants to know who you are!'

The Grand Ballroom was buzzing with expectation as Walter and Hellerman entered through a side door, unseen by the world leaders and dignitaries, who occasionally glanced towards the main entrance in anticipation of Walter's arrival. Hellerman nodded in the direction of a table where Secretary Casserina sat with a tanned, grey-haired man who was telling jokes but getting very few laughs in return.

'That's our President,' said Hellerman quietly.

'I know,' said Walter. He looked just like he did on TV – a cowboy without a hat.

Secretary Casserina was the first to spot Walter. Her eyes lit up as she rose to her feet and led the room in a standing ovation.

Walter forced a smile, he was a showman after all, and he had appeared on TV more times than he cared to remember as **Retlaw Dubelzaeps**, the backwards-spelling king. However, as Hellerman led him proudly through the room and on to the stage, he felt like a child lost in a crowd. Walter wished Harry was with him and felt a pang of disappointment that he hadn't been waiting for him when he came back.

Hellerman tapped the microphone with the palm of his hand. 'Boom, boom,' it sounded. He politely asked the dignitaries to sit down and, pointing to Walter, he spoke with the passion of a gospel preacher. 'World leaders and Mr President,' he began. 'We needed a saviour and a saviour came!'

Once more, the dignitaries rose to their feet in applause. Walter stared at his shoes.

'This boy . . .' continued Hellerman, taking Walter's hand and holding it above his head, 'this boy once risked his young life to travel to the moon to make the great dream come true.'

Walter felt idiotic and tried to pull his hand away, but Hellerman's grip was vice-like.

'Now he has volunteered to return to the past again and risk his life to save our planet!'

Again, the sound of applause filled the ballroom.

Hellerman gestured for silence. 'Our hero has had a long day and I cannot ask him to stay much longer. However, I will ask him to answer a question from the President of the United States of America.'

Hellerman looked at Walter, his expression demanding a positive reply. Walter nodded nervously. Hellerman stepped back from the microphone as Walter took his place.

The President stood up, holding a piece of paper in his hand. He cleared his throat then uttered one single word:

'Supercalafragalisticexpealadocious.'

Much chatter followed as the translators attempted to explain the word to the non-English-speaking delegates.

'S-u-o-i-c-o-d-a-l-a-e-p-x-e-c-i-t-s-i-l-a-g-a-r-f-a-l-a-c-r-e-p-u-s,' said Walter, spelling the word backwards in a flash.

The President checked the spelling against what was written on the piece of paper. 'Holy buckaroo!' he shouted. 'The kid is right!'

As he walked Walter down the corridor to the elevator Hellerman took a portfolio from his briefcase. 'All the information you need for your mission is here,' he said as he handed it to Walter. 'A map, the precise coordinates of where the UFO actually touched down, notes on what to do, and a letter from Al, which he wants you to give to his father, the First Contact Ambassador. Meet me and Secretary Casserina in the dining room at seven-thirty in the morning for an intensive briefing session before your eight-thirty departure. Share prices are falling on the stock exchange, Walter, and if you can get the job done before Wall Street opens in the morning you'll save the economy billions of dollars.'

'I'll look over the notes before I go to bed,' Walter replied, then he said goodbye to Hellerman, stepped into the elevator, took out his phone and texted Levon. '*Erahs secirp*! *Llaw teerts*! *Nialpxe*!'

He checked his watch. It was 6 p.m. New York time, which meant it was 11 p.m. at home but, knowing Levon, he would probably be under the covers with a flashlight, stuck into some book he couldn't put down.

Before the elevator stopped at the fortieth floor, Levon had already texted back. 'Buying shares like betting on d horses. U gamble ur money dat a company's share will do well. If yes u win if no u lose. Wall St is d stable.'

Walter turned his key in the lock and entered the room. 'Dad,' he called out excitedly, but there was no reply. He dropped his bag on the floor, then looked around the room. There was no sign of his dad's canvas bag. At times like this he wished that his dad had a mobile phone! Then he noticed that the balcony door was ajar.

'Hi,' said a voice from behind but, before he had time to look around, his body had left the ground, spun 360 degrees and landed with a soft thud on the carpet. His eyes were closed – they must have closed mid-spin – and when he opened them again he found himself staring at a pair of cowboy boots. He looked up to see a very familiar and pretty face.

'Annie!'

'Those who are not prepared are easy prey,' she said with a big smile.

Still dazed, Walter allowed Annie to help him to his feet. 'How . . .?' Walter began but he couldn't finish the sentence.

'Dad had to come to New York,' said Annie, running her fingers through her spiky blonde hair. 'There's been an emergency on the stock exchange and his business colleagues called an emergency meeting. Mum was away so he had no choice but to bring me!'

Walter struggled to take it all in. 'How . . . how did you get into the room?'

'I climbed over the balcony partition from next door. You forgot to lock the glass door.'

'You're next door?' he said.

'I asked Dad if we could stay here,' said Annie. 'He likes posh hotels! We asked for a suite next to yours and, for a very big tip, Finnegan arranged it! I've a hunch you're going to need some help.'

'Right now everything is hunky-dory, but I'm glad you're here!' said Walter. He took some iced water from the fridge, poured a glass for both of them and sat down opposite Annie. 'I want to tell you what's happened so far,' he said.

As he explained the events of the past two days, Annie's eyes grew wider and wider, but when he finished his story she said nothing. She seemed to have disappeared inside herself, just like she had done last year when he told her he was going to the moon.

When she finally spoke it was with a tone of deep concern. 'You're going back in time to try and save the lives of two aliens you've never met, with a three-minute window before you get blown up by an atomic bomb?'

'Two minutes and fifty-nine seconds to be exact,' said Walter.

The phone rang. Walter stared at it.

'It could be your dad,' said Annie. 'Aren't you going to pick it up?'

Something told Walter that it wasn't Harry. Something told him that the moment he answered the phone, things would change completely. His hand trembled as he picked up the receiver.

'Let's keep this very simple,' said a male voice with a distinctly foreign, accent.

The colour drained from Walter's face. Sensing something was wrong, Annie pressed the speakerphone button.

'I need one million in cash by sundown or you won't see your dad again. I'll call back with details of the drop. Have a nice day.'

Walter put the receiver back on the hook and stared at the wall. 'I'm not travelling back in time until I get my dad back!'

'I have a great idea!' said Annie, jumping to her feet. 'Just use your Giftstone to travel back in time to this morning before your dad was kidnapped.'

'Simple, but brilliant!' said Walter, reaching over and grabbing the canvas bag that lay on the floor beside him. He opened the flap and zipped back the inside pocket. 'That's strange!' he said. 'It was definitely here.'

'What?' asked Annie.

'The Giftstone.'

'It's gone?' said Annie.

'It *can't* be gone,' replied Walter.

'Turn it upside down,' said Annie. 'Empty everything out on the floor.'

Walter turned the bag upside down. A notepad, a couple of biros, a pair of sunglasses and a bottle of 'Toppup Red Herbal Hair Colourant' toppled on to the carpet.

'I thought your hair colour was natural!' said Annie. 'What a disappointment.'

'Oh no!' said Walter, shock bleaching the

colour from his face. 'I must have taken Dad's bag by mistake . . . and he's taken mine!'

Eht Noillim Rallod Pan

Walter paced the room while Annie sat curled up on the couch, deep in thought. There was a knock on the door.

'Open up.'

'It's Hellerman,' said Walter.

There was a jangling of keys, then the door opened and Hellerman marched in looking very unhappy.

'My dad!' cried Walter.

'I know,' snapped Hellerman, using his hand to indicate that Walter should be silent. 'All telephone conversations in this building are being tapped by us.'

'This is . . .' said Walter, looking around for Annie, but she had disappeared. He noticed that the balcony door was slightly ajar.

Hellerman raised an eyebrow. 'This is . . . what?'

'This is . . . terrible! I wish I had never come

to New York, Mr Hellerman! My dad has gone. My Giftstone has gone!'

'Your what?"

'My Ruby Giftstone and my *Book of Noitanigami*: I need the Giftstone to travel back in time. I had it in my bag but Dad took it by mistake.'

Hellerman's concern turned quickly to anger. 'Walter! I thought you had the power to reverse things and travel back in time at will. Now you tell me that you're just some child wizard who can't do a darned thing without his magic stone!'

Walter gritted his teeth. 'I can use **Noitanigami** to reverse living things and objects without the Giftstone, but I need to have the stone with me when I travel back in time. Now I want my dad back!'

Hellerman put his fingers to the centre of his forehead and closed his eyes. 'I'll need to put this to the UN Assembly. They're at dinner now, but I can have them return to the hall afterwards to discuss the issue. This is so embarrassing for me, Walter, you have NO idea!'

'Discuss the issue?!' shouted Walter. 'My dad's life and the future of the planet depend on the ransom being paid by sundown, but I don't have one million dollars!'

'Of course, I understand, Walter,' said Hellerman, his voice softening in an attempt to calm Walter down, 'but the President of the United States and the heads of the other nation states will have to approve it first. This is also a world security issue!'

'The kidnappers need the money by sundown, Mr Hellerman. There's no time for discussion. I want my dad back.'

Ignoring Walter's plea, Hellerman headed for the door. 'I'll update you when I have some news, Walter.'

As Hellerman shut the door behind him, Walter fell on to the couch and, despite his anger, jetlag soon caused his eyelids to become heavy. To try to stay awake, he jumped to his feet and performed some kung-fu kicks, but the moment he sat down again his eyes became even heavier and he soon drifted into a deep sleep. He awoke to find Annie sitting across from him fiddling with a coin. 'I found this out on the balcony,' she said. 'It's a foreign coin with a hole in it!' She handed it to Walter.

'It's one euro,' said Walter. 'That's not much use to us, we need to find one million dollars!'

'No worries!' said Annie, taking the coin back and placing it in her pocket.

'No worries?' said Walter, jumping to his feet. 'One million worries!'

Annie smiled and pointed casually to the rucksack lying on the ground beside her.

'Unless there is a million dollars in there,' said Walter, 'there's no reason to smile.'

'Guess what . . . there is!'

'Annie, I've got no time for funny stuff. My dad has been kidnapped!'

'You mean dad-napped!'

'Annie!'

Annie leaned over and opened her bag. Walter's eyes opened as wide as a flying saucer.

The bag was stuffed with large wads of hundred-dollar bills. He fell to his knees, took a bunch of wads in his hands, closed his eyes and shouted 'Hallelujah! Where the . . . where did you get this, Annie?'

'Good ol' Dad.'

'Your father gave you a million dollars for me? I've never even met him!'

'It's simple, Walter. The stock market has crashed. People like my dad have lost a lot of money, but if you save the world, the market will recover and my dad will make a lot of money – many, many millions of dollars! So giving you a million to pay the ransom is a sensible business decision.'

The phone rang. Walter stuffed the money back into the bag, jumped to his feet and pressed 'speakerphone'.

'De clock is ticking, buddy: tickedy-tockedy, tickedy-tock. You got de money?'

'Call me on my mobile,' Walter said. He gave him the number and hung up.

The mobile rang.

Walter answered, 'Where is the drop-off?'

'De crown balcony on de Statue of Liberty.'

'I've got the money. We'll be there by sundown.'

'One of my men will meet you there. He'll be smoking a cigar.'

'What about my dad?'

'You hand over de money, you get your dad.'

'No dad, no money,' said Walter.

'No money, no dad. I'm de boss here, kid, and don't you forget it.' The kidnapper hung up.

'The balcony in the crown is the best look-out tower in New York,' said Annie. 'Those kidnappers know what they're doing!'

'You've been there?'

'Every summer since I was five.'

'Will you . . . come with me?' Walter asked.

Annie smiled. 'Would you know how to get there on your own, Mr Adventurer?'

'Eh, no . . .'

The phone rang again. Something told

Walter it wasn't the kidnapper this time. He picked it up.

'Mr Hellerman?' he said politely.

'Do NOT deal with the kidnappers, Walter, and that's an order! We have teamed up with Detective Stark from the FBI who will launch a Triple Red investigation. Stark is the best in New York!'

'What about my dad?' asked Walter.

'We're following a definite lead, Walter. We have reason to believe that this is an inside job. We've got to do it our way. You'll get your dad back.'

'You can guarantee that?'

'There are no guarantees here, Walter. Kidnapping is a dangerous game.'

'But I want my dad back.'

Walter hung up the receiver.

There was a loud knock on the door followed by three more.

'Detective Stark, FBI. Open up.'

Annie grabbed her bag. 'Let's go,' she said, making for the balcony door.

'We're breaking down the door, Mr

Speazlebud! You've got ten seconds. 10-9-8 . . .'

Walter remembered that Hellerman had a key. If he wasn't already outside the door he was surely on his way. He ran to the door, slid the security chain across, then turned and followed Annie on to the balcony, snapping the sliding doors closed behind him.

'This way!' shouted Annie from next door.

Walter heard a tremendous crash coming from inside. Through a gap in the curtains he glimpsed cops and detectives scouring the room, kicking doors open, throwing their hands in the air. He climbed over the partition to where Annie stood waiting, and followed her inside, locking the door behind him.

'There's a utility stairway across the hall through the grey door,' she said. 'I'll go first, follow me.'

Annie walked to the door, unbolted it, eased it open and checked the corridor, left and right. She spotted an armed police officer patrolling the corridor. He had his back turned and was walking away to her right. She closed the door gently and listened for footsteps.

'He's taking about ten steps each side of your door,' she whispered, 'so when he passes in the direction of your room it gives us more time.'

She waited, then opened the door quietly, skipped across the hallway and through the open door of the utility stairway.

Walter waited for the footsteps to pass in the opposite direction. He counted them, opened the door slowly and stepped into the hallway. Then he closed the door gently behind him and tiptoed to the stairwell where Annie was waiting for him.

'We're walking all the way down?' he said with a grimace.

'It's the safest way. They can close down the elevators with the flick of a switch.'

From the hallway they could hear the sound of angry voices and more door-banging.

'This is the FBI. Open the door!'

'They're outside my door,' said Annie. 'Let's go.'

The sound of a door being kicked open jolted them into action and they began to descend the staircase two steps at a time.

'Hopefully they'll have the door fixed before Dad gets back from the opera!' said Annie.

Five flights down, they met a hotel maid carrying bed linen. Annie took a bar of chocolate from her pocket and handed it to the girl. 'You saw nothing.'

The maid winked. 'I see nothing.'

When they reached the basement, Annie pushed open a fire exit that led on to a cobbled alleyway. To the right, a cop guarded the exit to Park Avenue.

'This way,' she said.

Moving quickly in the opposite direction, they passed several alleyways until they came to one that was unguarded.

'The guard must be gone for a break,' said Walter.

'A lucky break,' said Annie, 'for us!'

They strolled down the alley and walked

casually on to the sidewalk.

'Cops!' said Annie, glancing right and left.

'Frankfurters!' said Walter, spotting a vendor on the sidewalk.

'No time for snacking,' said Annie, then she saw a yellow cab. 'Taxiiii!' she shouted at the top of her voice.

The taxi swung dramatically across the midtown traffic and jammed on its brakes, almost causing a pile-up behind. Annie clambered into the back, placing the bag securely between her feet. Walter hopped in beside her.

'Statue of Liberty ferry, South Ferry terminal,' Annie called to the foreign-looking driver.

'But you are only kids now,' said the driver, looking in his mirror. 'Where are your parents being?'

'I'm not a kid,' said Walter with a throaty growl. 'I suffer from Invertosemia, it's an illness that prevents ageing, and I don't appreciate you bringing it up. I'm actually forty years of age! This is my daughter Annie.'

Annie poked him in the ribs.

'A million apologies,' said the driver, 'and I mean no disrespect when I say that you could sell such an illness in the LA of California. There they are always obsessed with the eternal youth.'

In the wing mirror Annie spotted a police officer coming towards them. 'Duck, Walter – I mean Dad! It's you they'll be looking for. Can we go please, Mr Cabdriver!'

Walter ducked. Within seconds, the officer had reached the taxi and was bending over, staring through the window.

The car jerked into gear with a 'clunk and a 'vroom'! A toxic cloud of exhaust fumes enveloped the policeman, leaving him spluttering and gagging for air. The taxi edged its way into the downtown traffic.

'Did he see me?' said Walter.

'Probably.'

Walter uncurled himself and sat back in his seat, fear etched on his brow.

'Walter,' said Annie in her kung-fu teacher's voice. 'I want you to take a deep breath. Forget everything that has happened. Forget about your dad and Hellerman and the aliens and saving the world. Concentrate on what's happening now.'

Walter nodded.

The cab weaved its way towards the inside lane, throwing them from one side of the cab to the other.

Annie made a 'cup' with her hands. 'Put your fear in here,' she said.

Walter smiled. He hadn't done this exercise before.

'Put it here,' she repeated.

He pretended he was pulling an imaginary weed from the top of his head and placed it in her hands. She opened the window and 'threw' the fear out. He felt better immediately. Walter smiled across and Annie smiled back. Though things could not possibly be worse, he felt ridiculously happy and totally fearless.

Behind them they heard the sound of police sirens.

'Next right, on to 14th Street,' said Annie to the driver.

'OK. Hold on tightly if you please.'

As the driver swung on to 14th Street, Annie spotted a police officer on horseback up ahead. 'Stop,' she said, and the driver obeyed, making a loud skidding sound that caused the horse to rear, almost throwing the officer off. Walter and Annie looked at each other.

'What are you thinking, Walter?'

'I'm thinking that the city is no place for a hoss!'

The sound of helicopters overhead caused Annie to raise her voice. 'I'm thinking we haven't a hope of making it to the South Ferry by cab,' she said, as she pointed to a side street where the police had raised a barrier. Across the street, she spotted the entrance to 14th Street subway station. Annie slipped the bag on to her back, tightened the straps and opened the door. 'Get ready,' she ordered.

Walter handed the cabbie a twenty-dollar bill.

'Keep the change.'

'Thank you, sir, and do mind your daughter crossing the street.'

'I will,' said Walter, jumping from the cab and tailing Annie as she dodged through the traffic amidst the sound of horns blowing, brakes screeching, police sirens and hovering helicopters.

They entered 14th Street subway station and descended the stairway to the ticketing booth.

'Oh no,' said Annie, digging her hands into her pockets. 'I left my money in my other jeans.'

'And I gave that cab driver all my cash!' said Walter.

'We'll have to use the ransom money,' said Annie, sliding the bag from her back.

'Be careful,' said Walter as he noticed three teenagers – a small Latino boy, a skinny white boy and a chubby black boy – loitering by the turnstiles and glancing in their direction.

'Hold the bag,' said Annie, 'while I get the money out.'

She handed the bag to Walter, then began to undo the flap.

'Aaahhh!' screamed Walter, letting go of the bag, which dropped to the ground spilling wads of dollar bills on to the dirty concrete floor.

'Walter!' shouted Annie as, with lightning quickness, she dropped to her knees, gathered up the dollars and threw them back into the bag, keeping twenty dollars for tickets. From the corner of her eye she spotted a rat scurrying towards a drain with a piece of sandwich meat in its mouth. She smiled and then raised here eyes to heaven.

'Sorry,' said Walter with an embarrassed grin, 'but it's as big as a lamb.'

'It's just a New York rat,' she said as she threw the bag on to her back again. 'They own this city.'

The teenagers by the turnstiles were now huddled together in deep conversation.

'I hope they didn't see the money,' said Walter.

'We'll soon find out,' said Annie. 'Now, let's get our tickets and go.'

The 1 train was pulling into the station with an ear-melting screech of brakes as Walter and Annie reached the platform. The train stopped and the doors slid open. The driver's voice crackled from a faulty speaker. 'This is the one train to the South Ferry terminal. Christopher Street next stop.'

Walter and Annie stepped on to the train and grabbed the tubular handgrips for support.

'Stay clear of the closing doors,' said the driver.

They glanced around the crowded carriage. There was no sign of the teenagers they had seen by the turnstiles.

Seven stops later the subway slowed on its approach to the South Ferry. "Ding-dong!" The doors opened and Annie and Walter stepped on to the platform.

With that the teenagers jumped from the adjoining carriage. One grabbed the bag while the other two tried to wrestle Annie to the ground. Walter covered his eyes with his hands. He knew what was going to come next and he couldn't bear to watch. With a combination of lightning-quick hand movements, followed by three powerful kicks, the teenagers soon lay moaning on the platform.

'Those who are unprepared are easy prey,' said Annie as Walter removed his hands from his eyes.

'And those who are prepared are dangerous,' said Walter.

'Let's go,' said Annie.

They ran towards the stairway, through the turnstiles and out of the subway station. They were on the edge of Battery Park, with the Liberty ferry ticket office directly across the street. In the distance, the mighty statue was silhouetted by the setting sun. Walter took a moment to appreciate its towering beauty. It took a dig in the ribs from Annie to awaken him to the familiar sound of helicopters and police sirens.

'They're closing in again,' said Annie. She spotted a sycamore tree growing through the sidewalk, grabbed Walter by the arm and ducked in behind it. Soon a group of sightseers walked by and Walter and Annie casually stepped out from behind the tree and tagged along behind them. They crossed the street and as they headed towards the river Walter and Annie found the right moment to slip away down a grassy bank to a jetty. They crouched down.

The Circle Line ferry passed by, taking tourists on the sunset tour of Manhattan, then a speedboat – avoiding the ferry's wake – pulled into the jetty alongside them.

Annie didn't waste a second. 'Can you take us to Liberty Island?' she said to the tanned, young, speedboat driver.

'What? Two kids?' said the driver. 'Are you crazy?'

Annie reached into her bag and removed a one-hundred-dollar bill.

'Let's hope the kidnappers don't count it out in front of us,' she whispered to Walter.

'Pulling a one-hundred-dollar bill out of an old sports bag, now that's impressive!' said the boat owner. He took the money and turned to Walter. 'What's your party trick?'

'I can sing "Jingle Bells" backwards.'

'No way! That's outrageous. Are you some kinda freak or somethin'?'

'If I can do it,' said Walter, 'Annie gets her hundred dollars back and you take us to the island on full throttle.'

'Go for it, kid.'

Walter cleared his throat.

Elgnij slleb, elgnij slleb,
Elgnij lla eht yaw,
O tahw nuf ti si ot edir
No a eno esroh nepo hgiels.'

'Love it!' said the speedboat owner, handing back the hundred-dollar bill. 'You're the freak of the week! What's your name?'

'Walter and this is Annie.'

'I'm Kenny Carroll, captain of the New York City speedboat team.'

'Show us why they made you captain,'

said Annie as a helicopter appeared above the rooftops nearby.

'Jump in and fasten your seatbelts, kids!'

Hsad ot Ytrebil

As the speedboat bounced off the choppy waters of the Hudson, Walter and Annie closed their eyes and let the cool river mist wet their faces.

'Peace at last,' said Walter, but just then a helicopter appeared directly above them.

'Stop the boat!' said a voice blaring through a megaphone. 'Your passengers are under arrest.'

'What's going on?' shouted Kenny. 'You guys on the run?'

'Do something, Walter!' said Annie.

Walter took a deep breath and fixing an eagle gaze on the helicopter called out, '*Retpocileh, retpocileh, retpocileh.*'

The blades of the helicopter froze, like a snapshot in time, then began to rotate anti-clockwise. The helicopter reversed away, tracing its flight path backwards towards Manhattan.

'I thought "Jingle Bells" backwards was

impressive,' said Kenny, 'but that was awesome!'

Annie gave Walter's arm a squeeze. 'Your grandad would be proud.'

Walter smiled. 'Hopefully Harry will be too,' he said. 'Wherever he is right now, he'll have seen the Giftstone glow in the bag. He'll know we're on our way with the ransom.'

Minutes later, they reached Liberty Island, where Kenny dropped Walter and Annie in a quiet cove and wished them good luck. The statue's mighty shadow made for good cover as they ran across the grass and hid behind one of the trees near the entrance to the statue. Through the glass doors they could see security guards hovering about, speaking on their cell phones, primed for action.

'They've been tipped off,' said Annie. 'If we buy tickets we'll be nabbed.'

'Whatya sayin', pardner?' said Walter. 'One false move and the game is up?'

Annie nodded. 'And I'll be doggone if the law is gonna stop us now,' she said. 'Let's go.' Annie crouched down and, once the coast was clear, moved swiftly towards the rear of the statue with Walter close behind. There were several emergency exits, all locked, apart from one which had been left slightly ajar. Annie moved to the door and had a peek inside. She turned to Walter and whispered, 'It's the staff kitchen. The door was left open to dry the floor.'

'Is the coast clear?'

'Almost. There's a little old lady loading cups into a dishwasher.'

With a hand signal from Annie, Walter followed her through the door on his tiptoes. They snuck around the lady towards a door marked 'exit', which they quietly opened. A sign in the hallway pointed to the stairs.

They climbed up to the second floor and waited for the elevator. As they stepped in, they saw, through the glass windows, security guards beneath them in the foyer, checking all visitors for ID.

'Phew!' said Annie. 'Another close call.'

'Top floor. Liberty crown balcony,' said the recorded announcement as the elevator door opened. Walter and Annie stepped from the elevator on to a semi-circular metal balcony.

In the distance the skyscrapers of lower Manhattan were illuminated by soft evening light.

'Look,' said Walter, pointing to a police speedboat arriving in the harbour below. 'We don't have much time.'

'Where is our man?' said Annie, looking at the small group of sightseers standing nearby watching the sun disappear over the horizon.

A dark-clad figure appeared from the far end of the balcony and sidled towards Walter and Annie, stopping just yards away. He leaned over the railing. In the encroaching darkness, it was impossible to see his face. 'Drop the bag and don't try anything funny,' he said.

'Where's my dad?' said Walter.

The pick-up man struck a match and lit a cigar. The flame was reflected in the metal earring he wore in his left ear. He pulled heavily on the cigar and flicked the match to the wind.

'You'll get your dad back when I get my money.'

In the distance, Walter spotted another helicopter heading in their direction. He could use his **Noitanigami** again, but reversing a second helicopter might weaken his powers and make it difficult for him to time travel in the morning. They had to move quickly.

Sensing what he was thinking, Annie slid the bag from her shoulders and dropped it to the ground.

'Move away!' shouted the man in black.

Walter and Annie shuffled back along the balcony. The sound of the helicopter grew louder and louder.

'Where's my dad?' shouted Walter as the helicopter appeared in front of them as if it were projected on to a giant movie screen. The other sightseers ran from the balcony and on to the stairwell to avoid being blown off by the wind turbulence from the helicopter's blades.

'Get down!' shouted Annie as she and Walter dropped to the floor and huddled together, holding on to a metal beam.

'Those cops are crazy,' said Walter.

The elevator door opened and a police officer ran towards them. 'Do not hand over the ransom!' he shouted. It was Officer Shelley, who had greeted Walter and Harry at the airport.

'Too late, Officer Shelley,' said Walter as the officer crouched down beside them.

'Hellerman knows who the kidnappers are!' Shelley roared over the sound of the helicopter.

'He does?" said Walter. He turned around but the bag was gone, and so was the kidnapper.

'Maybe the helicopter crew saw where he went,' said Annie to Shelley.

Shelley looked at the helicopter, which was now moving away rapidly from the balcony. 'That's not one of our helicopters!' he said.

'It's him,' shouted Walter, spotting the man in black climbing the last rung of a rope ladder towards the helicopter, with Annie's bag on his back.

Shelley drew his gun but it was too late. The helicopter quickly disappeared out of sight.

A Yzarc Pu-xim

Walter barely noticed the skyscrapers glowing like giant lanterns beneath him as they flew back over the city in the FBI Special Task Force Helicopter. His mind was elsewhere, looking for the answers to some serious questions – would he ever see his dad again and could he still save the world?

Beside him, Annie sat enchanted by the view, despite the fact that she had just given away one million dollars of her father's cash. 'That's Broadway over there,' she said, pointing to a strip of dazzling neon that defined New York's famous theatre district.

Walter didn't hear a word she said but, sensing his state of mind, she placed the palm of her hand in front of him. He smiled, then 'plucked' the fear from the crown of his head and placed it in her hand. Annie took a deep breath then 'blew' the fear away. Walter laughed and poked her gently in the ribs. He was so glad to have his friend by his side.

'This is no laughing matter,' said Shelley, who was sitting directly behind them and fuming with anger. 'Hellerman has something to tell you, Walter, something that will knock that smile right off your face.'

Shelley escorted Walter and Annie from the landing pad on the roof of the Waldorf Astoria Hotel back to Walter and Harry's room, where he handed them over to Hellerman.

'Good work, Shelley,' said Hellerman. 'You can now go home and get some rest.'

'I want to know where my father is and when I can see him again!' pleaded Walter. 'We've paid the kidnappers –'

'Against government instructions,' snapped Hellerman. 'Were it not for the mission that awaits you, Walter, you would be in jail.'

'Were it not for the fact that I don't have my

Giftstone,' said Walter, angrily, 'I would travel back in time and say no to your stupid invitation to come here in the first place!'

Annie squeezed his arm. 'Take a deep breath.'

Hellerman gritted his teeth. 'And sit down,' he barked.

Walter took a deep breath and sat down on the couch beside Annie.

'Where did you get the money, Walter?' said Hellerman.

Walter continued to breathe deeply, but said nothing.

Hellerman spoke into his walkie-talkie, then smirked as he turned to Walter. 'I've got somebody for you to meet.'

The door opened, and a small bald man with bushy grey eyebrows walked in.

'This is Detective Stark, head of the FBI Triple Red Investigations squad, and he knows where you got the money from.'

'You got the money from Piper Zuckers,' said Detective Stark.

Walter had the look of a baby rabbit caught in the headlights of a truck. 'It . . . it was my idea to pay the ransom,' he said. 'Annie just helped me to raise the money.'

'Then you're the "innocent" one, Walter,' sniggered Hellerman. 'You need to wake up and smell the coffee.' He spoke into his walkie-talkie. 'Bring in the chief suspect, please.' He turned to Walter. 'Now you'll see who your friends really are!'

The door opened and a tanned, fit-looking, middle-aged man wearing a black suit and tie was escorted in by two police officers.

'Dad!' said Annie, jumping to her feet.

'Mr Zuckers?' said Walter. He had never seen the millionaire before.

'I thought you were at the opera, Dad,' said Annie.

'He was until Stark's men stormed the opera house and arrested him,' laughed Hellerman. 'Sit down, Miss Zuckers. You must not approach the accused.'

'The accused?' said Annie, reluctantly returning to her seat while continuing to stare at her father. 'What is going on, Dad?'

Piper Zuckers just stared at his feet.

Walter was confused.

'Your father has decided to stay silent until he speaks to a lawyer,' said Hellerman to Annie. 'He has asked that you do the same.'

'I haven't done anything wrong,' said Annie, 'and neither has my dad.'

'Hmmm,' said Hellerman, rubbing his chin. 'Let me spell it out for you, young lady. Your father is being charged with masterminding the kidnapping of Harry Speazlebud.'

'What are you talking about?' gasped Annie.

Hellerman made a hand gesture in the direction of the detective.

Stark cleared his throat. 'My Triple Red investigation has led me to believe that your father came to New York to kidnap Harry Speazlebud.'

'That's crazy!' said Annie. 'My father came here on business –'

Stark interrupted her, turning his gaze towards Walter. 'Piper Zuckers kidnapped Harry Speazlebud, knowing that you would not travel back in time until he was found, thus sending the stock markets crashing and allowing him to buy cheap shares. His plan was to sell the shares when the world was saved, at a much higher price, thereby making many millions of dollars in the process –'

'If he was the kidnapper,' interrupted Walter, 'why would he give me one million dollars to pay the ransom?'

'Wake up, Walter!' repeated Hellerman. 'By giving you a million dollars Piper Zuckers looks like the hero but, the fact is, he's paying the money to himself!'

Walter could barely take it all in. 'I . . . I don't believe you,' he said.

'You won't believe this either,' sniped Hellerman. 'His daughter is in it with him. She's his right-hand woman. Boy, this Annie Zuckers has really taken you for a mug!'

Walter looked at Annie. What Stark and Hellerman were saying was simply impossible. Annie was one of his closest friends, one of the people he trusted most in the world.

Annie returned his glance, searching in his eyes for any hint that he might believe them.

Hellerman muttered something into his walkie-talkie, then spread his hands in a grand theatrical gesture. 'And now, ladies and gentlemen, I am proud to present yet another prime suspect! You're gonna love this one! The man with the inside information, the man who made this crime possible . . . ta-da!'

'Oh, this is a terrible situation altogether,' said a voice from outside.

Hellerman danced comically towards the door and opened it.

'Finnegan!' said Walter and Annie simultaneously.

'In the name of God and all his holy saints, what are yis doin' to me?' Finnegan said as he was escorted through the door and stood beside Piper

Zuckers. 'Yis can't drag an innocent man from his bed like he was a crinimal.'

'Criminal,' corrected Hellerman.

'We have good reason to believe,' said Detective Stark to Walter, 'that Finnegan here provided the vital information that allowed Mr Zuckers and his daughter to carry out this unforgivable crime.'

'You're all crazy,' said Finnegan. 'I knows nuthin' and I does nobody no harm.'

'If you remember,' said Hellerman, 'Finnegan placed a certain gnome on your table when you and Harry arrived yesterday.'

'My lovely leprechaun!' said Finnegan. 'I won't have ya callin' him a gnome!'

Walter looked at the table. The leprechaun was gone.

'It is currently being examined,' said Detective Stark. 'I have reason to believe that the gnome is a bugging device Finnegan used to eavesdrop on yesterday's meeting. On first examination, we discovered *wires* inside.'

'Wires?' said Walter.

'Sure, there was wires inside the leprechaun,' said Finnegan. 'His eyes used to light up, and he'd sing an oul' song. The wires is only for connecting to the battery.'

'Likely story,' scoffed Hellerman. 'Chances, are, Finnegan, you'll never see your beloved Ireland again, or your ugly gnome for that matter. We're gonna lock you up and throw away the key.'

'You have the wrong man,' protested Finnegan, 'as sure as there's three leaves on the shamrock, as sure as country butter is the colour of the sun setting over the wesht.'

'I'm the Head of Operations at the CIA', scoffed Hellerman. 'I know what I'm talking about.'

'Then tell me where my father is!' said Walter. 'Why haven't you found him?'

Hellerman folded his arms. 'Because Mr Zuckers here is refusing to tell us where he is.'

It was all too much for Walter, and had it not been for Annie's comforting hand on his arm he would have broken down in tears. Then he heard the sound of keys being inserted in the door. He wasn't the only one.

'Who's there?' shouted Hellerman. 'Identify yourself or my officers will open fire.'

'Oh, an open fire would be lovely,' said the voice outside the door. 'I feel like putting my feet up.'

The door opened.

'Dad!' said Walter, running to the door and throwing his arms around Harry.

'Don't shoot,' said Hellerman to his officers. He turned to the detective. 'Stark, your men have obviously done a very fine job. They have released Harry Speazlebud from the hands of his kidnappers.'

'What kidnappers?' said Harry, while Walter dried his tears of joy with a paper handkerchief.

'The ones who kidnapped you!' said Walter.

'Don't be silly! I wasn't kidnapped!'

'What?' said Hellerman.

'I was at the da Vinci Exhibition at the Metropolitan Museum!'

'But it's ten o'clock and you've been gone all day,' said Walter.

'Oh, well, you see, just before the museum closed I had a brainwave,' said Harry. 'I needed to write my ideas down before they disappeared from my head and that's when I discovered that I had taken *your* canvas bag by mistake. As I didn't have my notepad, I went to the toilet to write on the loo paper. It's an old trick I learned in college when money was tight. So, I began to write and before I knew it I found myself locked in! It was just after five, and I had thought that the museum didn't close until five-thirty, but I obviously got it wrong! Four hours later, just as your Giftstone glowed in the bag a security man discovered me on his nightly round and let me out!'

Suddenly, Harry noticed Annie sitting in the armchair. 'What a surprise! How are you, my dear?'

'Well, apart from the fact that I have a million dollars less than I had earlier this evening, I'm great!' Annie replied.

Harry raised his hands to the heavens. 'I know, it's easy to get carried away when you go shopping in this city. I bought a couple of gizmos in the museum shop I'll probably never use.'

Piper Zuckers walked over to Hellerman and whispered in his ear, 'I want to use your "intelligence" to get me my money back, otherwise I'll sue you for false arrest and I'll have this sham all over the papers.' He turned to Annie. 'We should be going.'

Annie jumped up and winked at Walter. 'Good luck,' she said, then followed her dad through the door.

Walter felt funny watching her leave, but he had a strong feeling that he would see her again soon. He turned to Hellerman. 'If the kidnappers did not kidnap my dad, then who did they kidnap?'

Hellerman looked highly embarrassed. 'I'm afraid that I cannot answer that question right now, but with Stark's help, be assured we will attempt to find out.'

There was a knock on the door. 'Lab,' said the person on the other side.

Hellerman opened the door. A woman wearing a white coat walked in holding Finnegan's leprechaun.

Finnegan did a little Irish dance to express his joy. 'How are ya, me oul' segosha?' he said to the leprechaun. 'I hope they treated ya well.'

'Hi-tech bugging device?' said Hellerman to the woman.

The laboratory technician smiled, then she turned the leprechaun upside down and pressed a button. The song 'When Irish eyes are smiling' began to play, as the leprechaun's eyes lit up like Christmas lights, and Finnegan sang along at the top of his voice.

Hellerman grabbed the leprechaun from the lab technician and handed it to Finnegan. 'Take your noisy gnome and leave, before you drive me insane,' he said, then he grabbed a bottle of whiskey from the drinks cabinet and poured himself a shot to steady his nerves.

Finnegan turned the music off. 'I won't sleep a wink now after all this,' he said as he hugged his leprechaun. 'Being accused of a crime could have a terrible bad effect on an oul' creater like me, a man whose nerves was never the best . . .'

Hellerman took a hundred-dollar bill from his wallet and handed it to him. 'Please go, Mr Finnegan!'

'And a glass o' that whiskey,' said Finnegan, eyeing up the bottle on the shelf.

Hellerman sighed loudly, grabbed the whiskey and a glass and poured Finnegan a small measure.

Finnegan took the glass and examined it. 'Shur, that's not enough whiskey to make a baby burp.'

Hellerman threw another measure into the glass.

'Slainte,' said Finnegan, then he swigged back the whiskey, and made for the door.

'You go, too,' Hellerman bellowed at Stark. 'Find out who was kidnapped and who the kidnappers are.'

Stark was making his way to the door when he had a brainwave. 'Finnegan,' he said.

Finnegan, who had just reached the door, turned around with a scowl.

'Who was in this room before Harry and Walter Speazlebud?' asked Stark.

'That nashty young Greek multi-millionaire eegit, Poppadopolis,' said Finnegan.

'What are you getting at, Stark?' asked Hellerman. 'It better be good!'

Stark's eyes lit up.

'I have it! It was the millionaire who was kidnapped! His kidnappers rang his room looking for a ransom from his son, not knowing that the room had been taken over by the Speazlebuds. So, when Walter answered the phone they thought he was Poppadopolis's son.'

'I'm impressed,' said Hellerman. 'It's good to know that we're not paying you all that money for nothing.'

'Rubbish,' said Finnegan. 'Shur, didn't I see the Greek millionaire, his son and one of his cronies earlier today when I was callin' a taxi for Harry.'

Hellerman shook his head. 'I thought we were on to something, Stark. You'll have to try harder, much harder.'

The detective grabbed his briefcase and sheepishly followed Finnegan through the door.

'The Giftstone!' said Walter, turning to Harry. 'It's in the bag, Dad – the one you took to the museum.'

'What bag?' said Harry.

'My bag, the one you took by mistake!'

'Oh, *that* bag!' Harry looked at the ground to see if he had absent-mindedly put it down. 'I was sure I had it with me on the way back to the hotel.'

'Oh no, my bag has been stolen!' cried Walter.

Hellerman put his head in his hands.

The phone rang. Walter grabbed it and put his finger to his lips. There was a hush in the room. He pressed 'speakerphone.'

'We have your bag,' said a man with a foreign accent.

'Keep them talking,' whispered Hellerman.

'How much?' said Walter.

'How much what?' said the voice.

'How much is the ransom?'

'No ransom!' Hellerman shouted.

Walter put his hand over the mouthpiece.

'We want the bag back, don't we?' he said to Hellerman, then he spoke once more into the mouthpiece. 'Tell us your price.'

'I'm sorry, sir, I don't understand. The bag is in reception. Mr Speazlebud left it in the cab outside the hotel. We'll send it right up.'

Walter hung up, his face a mix of joy and dread. Now he would finally have to go back in time and Annie wasn't here to blow his fear away.

Hellerman took another gulp of whiskey. 'We're back in business.'

Harry looked a little confused. 'Is there something going on that I don't know about?'

'Dad,' said Walter, 'I've decided to do it. I'm going back in time.'

Harry smiled. 'You might not have to, Walt.'

Tilnoom Snoitagitsevni

Harry unravelled the toilet paper, which was covered in notes and diagrams. 'I believe that I'm close to discovering the secret of the aliens' mass displacement inversion technology,' he said.

Hellerman gasped.

'Those four hours that I was locked in the loo made all the difference!' Harry said.

'You mean that your invention may allow us to divert Hellvega from its collision course with the earth?' Hellerman asked.

'I think so,' said Harry, 'but I'd like to get Dr Hardy's opinion.'

Hellerman called Dr Hardy on the hotel telephone and told him about Harry's breakthrough, then he pressed 'speakerphone'.

'I'm intrigued to hear what you've come up with, Mr Speazlebud,' said Dr Hardy.

'Well,' said Harry, 'I believe that we can

mimic their technology by sending a small relay satellite on board an Atlas 10 rocket. When the satellite lines up with both Hellvega and a particle-beam accelerator, located at the earth's equator, it should create a negative resonant magnetic response in the vicinity of the asteroid, thereby causing the asteroid to essentially become a black hole and swallow itself.'

'We . . . we never considered parking a particle-beam accelerator at the equator,' said Dr Hardy. 'It sounds fantastic, but I'll have my project director simulate your invention on computer right away and see what he comes up with.'

Hellerman hung up. Ten minutes later, the phone rang again. It was Dr Hardy. Hellerman nodded then said goodbye.

He turned to Walter. 'It looks like we won't need you to go back in time after all! Your dad has discovered the basic secret of the aliens' mass displacement inversion technology!'

Harry clenched his fists in joy. Now his son would not have to risk his life. Walter's brain told him that it was time to rejoice too, but, instead, his heart sank and his tummy did a flip. 'If I don't go back in time,' he pleaded with Hellerman, 'Al the alien's parents won't be saved!'

'You may be concerned with resurrecting two aliens,' said Hellerman, 'but I'm more concerned with saving the world!'

It had been a long, long day but when Walter finally got to bed he couldn't sleep a wink. He tossed and turned, then switched on the bedside light and began to read the notes Hellerman had given him for his trip, and which he would no longer need. He imagined what it would have been like to see a real UFO land in the desert. He imagined what it would have been like to save the lives of Al the alien's parents. He silently recited Grandad's poem in an attempt to clear his mind.

This gift so rare
Given to you
Can make a million dreams come true

Can stop the arrow-head of time
And send it back, for you and yours
To do the things you might have done
To win the battles you might have won
To right a wrong, or simply be
A witness to Man's history.
When spoken with the power of truth
That nestles in the heart of youth
This gift will cast a blinding light . . .
Then every man will surely see
The power of **Noitanigami**.

He wanted to cast that light once more. He had been ready . . . then Harry had come along with his genius invention!

To calm his mind, Walter decided to go for a wander down the corridors of the hotel. At home, when he couldn't sleep, he would often walk down to the fields and wait for the dawn chorus to thrill his senses, but he wasn't going to wander around the streets of New York at 2 a.m.! He got dressed and grabbed his canvas bag, checking the pockets to make sure that he had the right one this time. He wasn't going anywhere without his Giftstone and *Book of Noitanigami*! He quietly left his room, crept past Harry's room, opened the door and ran straight into a police officer.

'I j-j-just . . .' stuttered Walter.

'Walter Speazlebud?' said the guard.

Walter nodded. 'I just want to go for a walk.'

'No problem. Your security status has been de-classified. I'm here to guard your father. You can go where you want.'

Walter felt a great sense of freedom as he wandered through the hotel. He also had a strange feeling that he was not alone, that he was being guided gently through the maze of corridors by an invisible hand. At the end of one corridor he noticed a large open window through which he could see the waxing moon float above the city. As he walked towards the window he heard somebody whistling a tune. He recognised it . . . it was the tune that Finnegan and his leprechaun had been singing – 'When Irish eyes are smiling'.

He stuck his head through the window.

'Annie!'

She was sitting cross-legged beneath him on the fire escape, the soft moonlight illuminating her face. 'I thought you might stumble by!' she said, turning to meet his gaze. 'You can't sleep either?'

'Too many things in my head.'

'Climb over,' she said. 'It's nice down here.'

Walter climbed through the open window, dropped on to the fire escape and hunkered down beside her. Though it was early morning, the city below was humming with life. He told her about Detective Stark thinking that the Greek tycoon Stavros Poppadopolis may have been kidnapped and then being proved wrong by Finnegan, but he couldn't bring himself to tell her that Hellerman had told him not to travel back in time.

'I think your dad *was* kidnapped,' said Annie.

'No,' said Walter. 'He was just locked in the toilets. He said so.'

Annie reached into her pocket, removed something small and handed it to Walter. He turned it towards the moonlight to get a better look.

'It's the coin with the hole in it,' he said. 'The one you found on the balcony.'

'It's a Greek euro,' said Annie.

'Maybe it belongs to Poppadopolis.'

'Maybe, but look at the hole,' she said. 'It's not in the centre and there's a metal ridge on one side of the coin.'

'Yes, Detective Zuckers?' said Walter, raising an eyebrow. 'What can it all mean?'

'It means it's a bullet hole,' said Annie. 'Dad said that when a coin like this is sent to somebody it means "leave the country now or there's a bullet with your name on it on the way".'

'You think that somebody sent it to Poppadopolis?'

Annie nodded. 'And if they did, it means that he's not just a Greek tycoon but a Greek tycoon mixed up in crime. It means he's in America because he's afraid to return home.'

'Why would he be carrying it around?' Walter asked.

'Dad reckons it's because if anything bad happens to him, the police will know who did him and be able to trace his killers.'

'How?'

'The bullet hole. Every gang uses a different kind of bullet, like a trademark.' She took a Blackberry from her bag and switched it on. 'It's my dad's. He doesn't need it when he's sleeping.'

She opened Google and began to type 'Stavros . . .' 'How do you spell Poppadopolis?'

'Do you mean backwards?'

'Yeah, whatever.'

'Haven't a clue!' said Walter.

She tried 'Stavros Popadoppless'. A message appeared onscreen. 'Do you mean Stavros Poppadopolis?' Annie clicked 'yes.'

A magazine article appeared, accompanied by a photograph of a tanned, chisel-featured young man lying by a swimming pool, wearing sunglasses and sipping a cocktail.

'I . . . I've seen that face before,' said Walter.

Annie looked up from the screen. 'Where?'

Walter clenched his fists and furrowed his brow, but the answer wasn't coming.

Annie returned to the screen and glanced through the article, picking out the important bits. 'He's into football, fast cars, girls and expensive hotels,' she said.

Walter shuffled nearer and looked over Annie's shoulder at the screen.

'He left Greece two years ago,' she continued, 'and moved to America, where he is said to have set up a security company.'

'Security?' said Walter as a little bell rang in his head, even if he wasn't sure why.

'His company is called Gold Security,' said Annie. 'There's a link.' She clicked on the link and read out the information at the top of their webpage. 'Gold Security. Providing security to the art world.'

'The photograph!' said Walter, looking at a shot of Poppadopolis wearing a suit and a big smile. 'That's him! That's the man I saw on the balcony across the street on the day I arrived.'

'Good,' said Annie. 'We may be getting somewhere.'

'What else does it say about Gold Security?'

'It says, "We provide 24-hour security for priceless masterpieces, private art collections and galleries."'

'Hmm,' said Walter, the alarm bells ringing louder in his brain. 'Galleries. Let's look at their client list for New York.'

'The Guggenheim Museum,' said Annie, 'the West Side Art Emporium, the Modern Masterpiece Museum, and the Metropolitan Museum of Art.'

She turned to Walter. 'We may have our man.'

'You're still a step ahead of me. How did you figure that out?'

'Walter, what happened to your dad at the museum?'

'He got locked in,' said Walter. 'It could happen to anybody.'

'Let's try their website,' said Annie, 'and check their opening times.' She typed in the words 'Metropolitan Museum'. The website popped up.

'Nine-thirty to five-thirty p.m., Monday to Thursday', she said.

'Dad said he thought that they were open until five-thirty,' said Walter, 'and he was right. But he got locked in at five past five!'

Annie looked Walter in the eye. 'Your dad *was* kidnapped,' she said. 'By one of Poppadopolis's security guys!'

Walter was taken aback. 'You mean they kidnapped him by locking him in the toilets?'

'Yes,' said Annie. 'And they released him once the ransom was paid. A perfect kidnapping! The victim didn't even know he had been kidnapped!'

'Why would Poppadolopop want to kidnap my dad?'

'As *my* dad said, "a man who has a bullet with his name on it is likely to be involved in crime" . . . Maybe his crime was kidnapping.'

Walter put his hand to his head. 'Maybe not,' he said. 'Maybe Poppolopolop left Greece because he owed money . . . a lot of money to the bad

132

guys, and he turned to kidnapping to pay back his debts. His security business is just a front for his kidnapping business.'

Annie nodded approvingly. 'He must have reckoned that if Harry could afford the Panorama suite he was a multi-millionaire, and worth kidnapping.'

'Exactly,' said Walter, 'and he was also angry because Hellerman asked him to leave so that me and my dad could move into the Panorama suite. So he decided to get revenge and make some money into the bargain.'

Annie returned to the magazine article with the photograph of Poppadopolis by the pool. 'There's one other person we need to find . . . and it shouldn't be too difficult.' She moved to the next page. It showed Poppadopolis throwing a jockey on to the back of a racehorse, Poppadopolis at a fashion show with a supermodel on his arm and Poppadopolis climbing into his private helicopter.

'Got him,' said Annie. She pointed to a suited man in the background of every photograph wearing sunglasses and an earring. 'Recognise the earring?' she said.

'Don't think so,' said Walter.

'Think again. Think flame and Statue of Liberty.'

'Got it!' said Walter. 'The pick-up man's earring at the Statue of Liberty. It's his bodyguard!'

'Yup, and I think you'll find that he has army training,' said Annie. 'Most of them do, at least the ones my dad uses when he travels to dangerous places do.'

'Right,' said Walter, 'and that's how he could pull a stunt like climbing the rope ladder to the helicopter.'

Annie gave Walter a high five. 'We should go into business together,' she said.

'We already are,' said Walter. 'The business of having fun.'

Annie laughed.

'Grandad used to say, "Life is the movie you see through your own eyes",' continued Walter. 'It always feels a bit like a movie when you're around.'

'What kind?' said Annie.

'A really good one!'

It was a few moments before Annie said anything. An aeroplane blinked in the sky.

'Thanks,' she said as a little tear escaped and ran down her face. She brushed it away quickly with her sleeve, then looked at her watch. 'It's ten past two, Walter. You have to travel back in time in less than five and a half hours.'

Walter took a deep breath, plucked the fear from the top of his head, placed it in his other hand and blew it away.

'Is there something you want to tell me?' asked Annie.

'Yes,' said Walter. 'While Dad was in "captivity" he invented a mass displacement inversion device which can be used to wipe out the asteroid. Hellerman doesn't need me to go back in time now!'

'But what about the aliens?' asked Annie.

Walter stared at the moon. 'That's why I couldn't sleep. Al the alien is expecting me to go back and save his family.'

135

'It does mean risking your own life, Walter.'

'But I'm the Keeper of the Giftstone, Annie. I promised Grandad I would use it to bring good to the world.'

'So you're going to do it?' said Annie.

'What would you do if you were me?' said Walter.

'I'd . . . follow my heart.'

'That's what I'm going to do,' said Walter.

'But it doesn't mean that you don't have to be careful!' said Annie. 'I want you to come back safely.'

Walter nodded. 'There's no time to waste,' he said. 'I want to have my mission finished before Hellerman wakes up.'

He reached into his bag, took out the wooden box and removed the Giftstone. He held it in his right hand until he felt its warm energy charging every cell in his body. He placed the stone back in the box and removed *The Book of Noitanigami*, along with Hellerman's instructions. He opened the book, turning it slightly to let the light of the moon fall on the page. Finding the chapter, '*Levart fo Emit*', he silently read his grandad's instructions. Walter then looked at the landing coordinates given to him by Hellerman. He closed his eyes and uttered the silent backwards spell.

Soon a small mist circle appeared, coming slowly towards him on a light breeze. He placed his hand gently on Annie's arm. 'Annie, I need you to meet Hellerman at eight a.m. in the dining room, and tell him what we know about Poppadopolis and his right-hand man. It should be all they need to arrest him and get your dad's money back. Tell him I've gone back to save those who wanted to save us from ourselves.'

'What about your dad?'

'I'll see him back in Nittiburg . . . tell him that if anything goes wrong to use his mass displacement inversion technology. At least the world will be saved . . .'

The mist circle drew closer and closer.

'You're really doing this for your granddad, aren't you?' said Annie.

Walter smiled. 'I couldn't do it without him.'

Annie leaned over and gave him a peck on the cheek, then the mist portal made contact with Walter's centre, just below his bellybutton. The Giftstone glowed brightly in the canvas bag, and Walter disappeared.

Walter found himself standing in the desert and feeling like he had just woken up. The sun was low in the sky, and the desert heat was made bearable by a light wind that shifted the golden sand around his feet. He stretched his limbs and yawned, took Hellerman's map from his canvas bag, examined it, folded it again and looked around him.

He saw the concrete building in the distance, marked as a bomb shelter on the map, the same building that would later become a prison – the prison where he had visited Al. He remembered reading in Hellerman's notes that the nuclear scientists and army chief of staff disappeared underground to avoid the shock waves and radiation, meaning Walter's presence would go unnoticed. He felt at ease on his mission, but one glance at the cylindrical metal structure sitting on a sand hill in the distance made him shudder. It was clearly marked on his map as the atomic bomb, and it would explode less than three minutes after the spaceship landed, which should be soon if Hellerman's instructions were correct.

Above Walter, beautiful birds of prey circled majestically against an azure blue sky. They, like all the living creatures for miles – apart from those in the bomb shelter – would be destroyed when the bomb exploded, and Walter would be too, if he did not make it back to the future in time.

As Hellerman's notes instructed, he searched the northern sky and soon spotted a flickering light just above the horizon. Suddenly it 'hopped' to another location, defying all rules of motion and gravity, just like the strange lights he had seen on his moon mission. The hopping stopped, and the light moved directly towards Walter until he could see that it was actually shining from the base of a saucer-shaped UFO, just like the photos he had seen in books. He took his camera phone from his pocket, put the viewfinder to his eye and took a snap. There was no sound as the strange object moved closer, its searchlight

The amazing photograph was taken by Walter Speazlebud as the alien spaceship came into view and less than one minute before it landed.

illuminating the desert beneath it. Then it stopped moving and hovered above the spot Hellerman had marked on the map, just one hundred yards from where Walter now stood.

He reckoned that the unidentified flying object in front of him was the size of an average one-storey house, so it surprised him that it sat so lightly on the sand when it landed, as if it were filled with helium gas.

Walter pressed the timer on his watch and ten seconds later a hatch opened upwards, metal steps dropped automatically to the ground and a silver-suited alien figure appeared at the doorway. This was the First Contact Ambassador, Al's father.

Walter walked towards the spaceship waving his hands. The ambassador continued down the steps and stood at the base of the ladder. Another figure appeared at the doorway – a woman, the alien's wife and Al's mother.

As he drew closer to the alien standing before him, Walter saw that familiar warm smile and felt the same giddy feeling he felt when he had first met Al.

'You must leave,' he said.

The alien replied in perfectly understandable English. 'But . . . we have come . . . to save your planet . . . from destruction.'

Walter removed Al's note from Hellerman's folder. It was written in the Assinian language. He handed it to the alien then he glanced at his watch once more: one minute and fifty-nine seconds to go before the bomb went off.

The alien read the note and, with a sense of urgency registering on his face, called to his wife and said something Walter could not understand. She disappeared and seconds later Al appeared at the doorway, looking no different than he did in the future. He climbed down the steps, took the note from his father's hand and read it. He turned to his father, said something, and kissed him on the cheek. A tear appeared in his father's eye, then he climbed the ladder and disappeared inside.

'You must go too, Zenon,' pleaded Walter, pointing to the bomb. 'It will blow up in one minute.'

'If you . . . can take the bomb away . . .' replied Zenon, 'I can stay.'

'Why?' said Walter with a puzzled look. 'Don't you want to return home with your parents?'

The alien pointed to the note. 'It says . . . that without me . . . the space programme will not advance so quickly . . . the 1969 moon landing . . . twenty-two years from now . . . will not happen . . . so you will not walk on the moon.' Then he looked with warmth and kindness into Walter's eyes. 'You have saved the lives of the ones I love . . . so I will sacrifice my life on Assina . . . to make both your dream – and the dream of mankind – come true.'

'But you are the captain of the spaceship!' Walter said.

'My father taught me how to be a pilot . . . he can fly the spaceship home.'

Walter was stuck for words. He glanced at his watch. He had thirty-five seconds left to pick a time in history, drop the bomb there, and get out before it blew up! He grabbed *The Book of Noitanigami* and flicked quickly to the section called '***Emit gnillevart htiw egral stcejbo***'. As he speed-read Grandad's writing, he felt the shadow of the UFO darken the earth as it rose silently into the heavens. He checked his watch. TWENTY-FIVE SECONDS LEFT! PANIC! His stomach muscles tightened. He stopped breathing. He thought he was going to pass out.

Then Grandad's voice appeared inside his head. 'Be brave, Walter, be brave.'

He breathed in, then plucked the fear from his head and threw it to the wind. He breathed out, concentrated deeply and, finally, with fifteen seconds left, a mist circle appeared before him, moving towards his centre. He took the Ruby Giftstone in one hand and reached out his other hand to Zenon. 'It was nice to meet you, Zenon,' said Walter.

Zenon took Walter's hand and squeezed it lightly. He looked once again at the note he held in the other hand and read, 'Our bloods may differ . . . but we are tied together . . .'

The mist circle made contact, the Giftstone glowed, and Walter disappeared.

Eht Hturt Tuoba Sruasonid

Harry and Peggy Speazlebud, Granduncle Bob and Gertrude Speazlebud and Levon and Annie stood silently and tearfully by a graveside covered in flowers. Harry put his arm around Peggy's waist, while Annie handed Levon a tissue from a packet, took one herself and dried her eyes.

Bob, who had his hands clasped together, was the first to find the words to express his feelings. 'He was special,' he said, and Gertrude showed that she agreed by squeezing his arm lightly.

'He was,' agreed Peggy, 'and we were so lucky . . . to have him in our lives.' She wiped her eye, then laid her head on Harry's shoulder and felt his comforting arm tighten around her waist.

'He was a couple of coupons short of a pop-up toaster,' whispered Levon and Annie tearfully agreed.

Just then a friendly rook flew over their heads and landed on the headstone. He lingered a moment, as if in prayer, before flying back to the rookery in the old chestnut tree nearby. At the foot of the chestnut, unseen by those at the graveside, a young man wearing a smart suit and dark glasses stood holding a bunch of beautiful blooming roses. As his family and friends left the graveside and made their way towards the gate, Walter removed his sunglasses and walked, for the first time, to his grandad's grave. He placed the roses at the foot of the gravestone, along with a note that read:

Rof ym devoleb dadnarg,
Dlonra Dubelzaeps.
A nam fo Noitanigami
dna a raed dneirf.
Uoy era dessim.

Walter stood for a moment in silence, then he leaned over and plucked one small red rose from

147

the bunch and stuck it in the buttonhole of his jacket. His spirits rose, like the moment he first put his eye to a telescope on a full-moon night, like when he took that one giant leap for mankind.

Just then, accompanied by the cawing of the rooks and the melody of the wind, he heard a familiar voice.

'*Ho ynaad yob, eht sepip, eht sepip era gnillac.*' It was the voice of Grandad Speazlebud singing his favourite song. Walter sang along until tears of joy ran down his face.

Nearby, one-eyed Sam the gravedigger stuck his head out of a hole in the ground. 'You did it, Master Speazlebud, by heck you did it!' he cried.

'So you saved the aliens' lives,' said Levon, wide-eyed, as he cycled with Walter down Nittiburg Hill, 'then you had to get rid of the bomb?'

'Al's life depended on it. The future of space travel depended on it!'

'How much time did you have?'

'Fifteen seconds.'

'Tight as a cowboy's belt, partner! What did you do?'

'I used my **Noitanigami** to send the bomb back in time to another period in history.'

'Cool!' said Levon. 'What period? The seventies?'

Walter smiled. 'Well, you know there are different ideas about how dinosaurs became extinct?'

'Yeah, some people think it was a giant asteroid and others think . . .' Levon's bike wobbled, almost causing him to crash into the pavement. 'You didn't!!!'

Walter nodded.

'You blew up the dinosaurs!' said Levon.

Walter nodded again.

'With an atom bomb!'

'They were extinct anyway,' said Walter, 'and you owe me one euro!'

Stnemegdelwonkca

Many, many thanks to Herbie Brennan and Jacquie Burgess, Brian Delaney, Paul Galbally, Brendan Harding, Alison Hearne, Nick Kelly, Sean Morgan, Aidan Ravitch, my agent Sophie Hicks, my elbagitafedni editor Cally Poplak and all the lufrednow folk at Egmont.

Did the **moon landing** really happen?

DAVID DONOHUE

MOON MAN

A quirky and wonderful world... the story is compelling and Walter is a wonderful creation
EOIN COLFER

One boy with

amazing abilities is going to find out!

Using the incredible power of **Noitanigami**

– and with his grandad's help –

Walter Speazlebud

will travel back to 1969 to discover the **truth.**

It's a **big** step for a small man...